the almost truth

Also by

EILEEN COOK

What Would Emma Do?

Getting Revenge on Lauren Wood

The Education of Hailey Kendrick

Unraveling Isobel

Used to Be

the almost truth

EILEEN COOK

SIMON PULSE

NEW YORK LONDON TORONTO SYDNEY NEW DELHI

This book is a work of fiction. Any references to historical events, real people, or real locales are used fictitiously. Other names, characters, places, and incidents are the product of the author's imagination, and any resemblance to actual events or locales or persons, living or dead, is entirely coincidental.

SIMON PULSE
An imprint of Simon & Schuster Children's Publishing Division
1230 Avenue of the Americas, New York, NY 10020
First Simon Pulse hardcover edition 2012

For information about special discounts for bulk purchases,
please contact Simon & Schuster Special Sales at 1-866-506-1949
or business@simonandschuster.com.
The Simon & Schuster Speakers Bureau can bring authors to your live event.
For more information or to book an event contact the Simon & Schuster Speakers
Bureau at 1-866-248-3049 or visit our website at www.simonspeakers.com.
Designed by Angela Goddard
The text of this book was set in Adobe Garamond.
Manufactured in the United States of America
2 4 6 8 10 9 7 5 3 1
Library of Congress Cataloging-in-Publication Data
Cook, Eileen.
The almost truth / by Eileen Cook.
p. cm.
Summary: When a teenaged con artist realizes that she looks like an age-enhanced photo of a missing child, she decides to pull the ultimate con—until she begins to suspect she may actually be the missing child.
ISBN 978-1-4424-4019-7 (alk. paper) ISBN 978-1-4424-4021-0 (eBook)
[1. Swindlers and swindling—Fiction. 2. Impersonation—Fiction.
3. Missing children—Fiction.] I. Title.
PZ7.C76955Al 2012 [Fic]—dc23 2011049870

To every English teacher and librarian
who gave me a passion for books, thank you.

chapter one

You know it isn't going to be a good day when you have to choose between food and proper hygiene.

"Can you take the milk off the bill?" I asked the cashier. My cell phone began to ring. I dug around in my bag for it.

"You don't want it anymore?" The cashier tapped her impossibly long fingernails on the register with one eyebrow raised.

"That's right. I don't want the milk," I repeated. This wasn't true. I wanted the milk. Eating dry cereal for a week was going to suck. Not to mention having so little dairy in my diet that I would likely end up with a raging case of osteoarthritis when I was old. But until my mom got paid on Friday, there were limited funds in the house, and there's no way I was going without deodorant. I finally found my phone buried at the very bottom of my bag and yanked it out.

"Sadie, it's Brendan." I didn't need him to tell me his name. Brendan has this habit of yelling into his cell as if it were a tin can on a string.

"Hey," I said. I looked at the new total on the register. *Shit.* "Can you take the toothpaste off too?" We'd have to squeeze a few more days out of the old tube. Now in addition to having brittle bones, I could be toothless. My future was looking brighter and brighter all the time.

The woman in line behind me gave an exasperated sigh. Screw her. She was probably one of those people who always makes you wait while they count out the exact change from their Coach wallet. I turned around. Great, it was Rebecca Samson and her mom. Their cart was piled high with groceries, including that expensive cheese made by yaks that costs something like twenty dollars for an ounce.

"Gosh, Sadie, do you need to borrow a couple dollars?" Rebecca asked, fighting to keep a smirk off her face. Her mom might have also been trying to smirk, but her face was so Botoxed she was incapable of expression.

"Hey! Is that Blow Job Becky I hear? What are you doing hanging with the cheerleader from hell?" Brendan bellowed. His voice carried out of my phone like he was on speaker. Rebecca's face froze as hard as her mother's.

"The total's twenty-two fifteen. How does that work for you?" The cashier tapped her fingernails again.

"Hang on, I'm at the store," I said to Brendan. I plunked my phone down on the conveyor belt and pulled some cash out of my bag. I made sure to spread the two twenty-dollar bills out in a fan shape so they could be clearly seen by the cashier and Blow Job Becky, too.

The cashier snapped her gum when she saw the money. No doubt she wondered why I had nickeled and dimed my bill when I had forty bucks. She handed over my change. I palmed the ten-dollar bill she gave me and, with my thumbnail, pulled a folded five-dollar bill from under my watchband. I made a show of counting the bills. "I'm sorry. I think you didn't give me enough change." I held out the two fives, a couple ones, and eighty-five cents.

The cashier screwed up her face. "I swore I gave you a ten. Sorry." She pulled another five out of the drawer and handed it to me.

"No problem." I tucked the money into my bag and took the groceries from her. An extra five bucks was going to come in handy. I could use it to buy milk, but I had more immediate needs than staving off osteoarthritis. I smiled at Rebecca and her Botoxed mom and stepped outside. As soon as the automatic doors closed behind me, it felt like I was slapped in the face with the hot, wet air. It might sound good in theory, but summer sort of sucks unless you can spend it sitting by the ocean with a fruity drink. Spending it in a parking lot with your T-shirt damp and sticking to you isn't that much fun.

"Sorry about that, you caught me in the middle of something,"

I said into the phone. I leaned against the warm cinder-block wall. A small kid was standing near me, staring at the pony ride next to the row of gum-ball machines. I tried to ignore him, but he looked like someone had shot his puppy. I sighed and handed him a quarter. He broke into a smile and climbed up on the mechanical horse, leaned forward, and fed the machine the coin. Ah, when joy could be purchased for less than a buck.

"Are you still running that wrong change con for five bucks?" Brendan said. "I keep telling you to up the ante. If you cashed in a hundred-dollar bill, you could easily clear twenty bucks."

"Twenty bucks is more likely to get noticed," I pointed out. "Not to mention if I start flashing hundred-dollar bills around town, that's going to seem weird."

"So you're doing the small con just to be careful? Are you trying to tell me it has nothing to do with the fact that if the short is less than five dollars, then the cashier doesn't have to pay it out of their own pocket?"

I dragged my sneaker on the cement. "Being a cashier at the Save-on-Food Mart is punishment enough. She doesn't need to cover me."

Brendan laughed. "Your ethics are getting in the way of the big score, but hey, it's your choice. What are you up to tonight? I was thinking we could go over to Seattle and grab dinner."

I snorted, knowing full well Brendan's idea of grabbing dinner. "You buying or is the restaurant?" I asked.

"Now why in the world would I pay?" Brendan wasn't teasing.

He actually was incapable of understanding why he should have to pay for anything when he was clever enough to steal it without getting caught.

"While stealing a meal with you sounds like an attractive option, I'm going to have to say no."

"For a con artist you have a highly overinflated sense of morals," Brendan said. "Especially when dinner is on the line. We could go for Japanese if you want."

"Don't call me that. Besides, you hate Japanese."

"Yet another good reason I shouldn't have to pay for it."

I rolled my eyes. If you wanted to get technical about it, I *was* a con artist. I'd learned the tricks of the trade from my dad. Then I taught what I knew to Brendan, who happened to have some sort of freakish natural ability in the area. He was like a con genius savant. However, unlike Brendan, who just loved getting away with something, I preferred to see it as a means to an end, an end that was finally coming to a close. "I can't go to dinner, I've got stuff to do tonight."

"Like what?"

Most people would take a polite brush-off and move on. Brendan was not most people. "I have stuff to get ready for school."

"You're not going away to college for months. C'mon, a night in the city would be fun."

I knew down to the exact day (sixty-four, counting today) how soon I would be leaving Bowton Island for college. If I were better at math, I would be counting down the hours in my head.

"I want to do some packing," I said. The truth was, it wouldn't take me that long to pack. My bedroom was the size of a closet. Even if I took the time to fold each item of my clothing into a tiny origami crane, there'd be no need to start now. The problem was spending time with Brendan felt weird lately. We'd known each other since we were kids, and on an island where 90 percent of the residents measured their wealth in terms of millions, and those of us in the remaining 10 percent measured it by having enough to buy groceries, we were automatic allies. Brendan had been my best friend as long as I could remember.

Brendan was the one who'd realized that the pranks I'd taught him could be used to pull cons to raise cash. He helped me figure out what I needed to do to escape my life. I would always owe him for that. The problem was, he didn't want me to leave. Or at least he didn't want me to leave without him, but where I was going there would be no room for him. I was planning to make over my entire life, and that meant leaving the old me behind.

Then there was the uncomfortable realization that Brendan maybe wasn't thinking of me as just his best friend anymore. There'd been a few awkward moments where I'd caught him staring at me, and at graduation I'd thought he might try to kiss me. And not in a "wow, we're great friends and we survived high school" kind of way.

"Maybe we could do it another time?" I asked.

"Fine, but you can't blow me off forever," Brendan grumped.

"I'm not blowing you off. I'm tired, that's all."

"Then get some sleep and we'll do it tomorrow night. No excuses." Brendan clicked off before I could say anything else.

I tossed my cell back into my bag. I pulled out the ten-dollar bill I'd dropped in there after palming it and stuck it in my wallet. Taking a five at a time wasn't adding up fast, but combined with the money from my part-time job at the hotel, it did add up. Brendan could tease me if he wanted, but I knew that while larger cons might pay off better, they also came with much bigger risks. My dad was a living, breathing example of that. For as long as I could remember, he had been in jail more often than he'd been out. I suspected the correctional officers knew him better than I did. One year when he was on probation, they sent him a birthday card.

For Brendan, the point was the con, not the cash. As soon as the money came in, it went right back out. I'd been stockpiling mine. In three and a half weeks I would put most of it down to hold my place at Berkeley. I was going to college, and I planned to leave all of this behind me.

The doors to the grocery swooshed open and Rebecca and her mom came out. Her mom pushed their cart past me as if I didn't even exist. I suspected she saw me like the help, best ignored unless she needed something. Rebecca glanced over at my Old Navy T-shirt and my cutoff shorts. Somehow she managed to look cool and unfazed by the heat. It was like being really rich also made her immune to humidity and the need to sweat.

"Nice outfit," she said, her smirk in full force.

"Aw, that would hurt my feelings if I cared about your opinion," I said. This was a concept Rebecca had never fully grasped. She felt everyone should want her love and approval. She was also open to ass kissing. It really chafed her fanny that I didn't care what she thought of me. It must have made her job as the popular mean girl so much less enjoyable when what she said didn't bother me. She was also apparently unaware of the fact that high school was now over, making her the queen bee of nothing. I noticed a glint of silver on her perfectly pressed polo shirt. "Is that your cheerleading pin?" I asked.

Rebecca fingered the silver megaphone. "It's my captain's pin."

I couldn't decide if it was merely sad or full-on pathetic that she was still wearing it postgraduation. Rebecca was going to grow up to be one of those overly skinny women who hang out at the country club bitching about how their husbands are never around, how their maids don't scrub the toilets to their satisfaction, and how high school was the best time of their lives. Personally, I was planning on my life getting better from this point forward.

I picked up my bag of groceries. "You have a good rest of the summer," I called over my shoulder at her as I walked away. Being nice to Rebecca would screw with her head more than any sarcastic comeback. I tucked my bag into the basket attached to the back of my scooter. Rebecca might mock my secondhand clothes and Brendan might make fun of my five-dollar cons, but in sixty-four days none of it would matter.

Unlike Rebecca, I didn't plan to look back on high school with fondness. I didn't plan to look back on it at all.

chapter two

You know what you never see embroidered onto a pillow? TRAILER, SWEET TRAILER.

Of course no one calls them trailers anymore. Now they're called modular housing. It's like how garbagemen are sanitation engineers, and instead of calling yourself short, you're vertically challenged. I never understood the point of all of that. Calling it modular housing doesn't change the fact that I live in a place that is basically a glorified tin can and can be moved by a really strong wind.

Bowton Island is made up mostly of multimillion-dollar estates for high-flying software executives who commute by ferry over to Seattle. When your house is called an estate, you can bet it doesn't tip over in a firm wind. Back in the early 1970s, a farmer who lived out on the very western tip of the island decided he was sick of raising sheep and instead set up cement slabs to create a trailer park. Now there are about two dozen trailers on the property. Most of the people who live in them work at the Keppler, the luxury hotel on the island. The trailer I share with my mom looks like it's sinking back into the earth. The once cream-colored siding is coated with dark olive algae due to all the rain. It needs to be power washed, but this requires both access to a power washer, and the motivation to do it, and we have neither. Our neighbor Ms. Flick keeps her place in immaculate condition, although she goes seriously overboard with the lawn ornaments. She loves those gnome statues. She has something like twenty of them sprinkled around her house. She also has two plastic geese that she dresses up to match the season. Currently they were wearing their Fourth of July outfits, bright red, white, and blue flag dresses. They were very patriotic geese. As I pulled up in front of our trailer, I could see Ms. Flick lying in her lounge chair in a bikini. Seeing a neighbor in a skimpy bikini is one thing, but Ms. Flick is over seventy.

I pulled my helmet off and yelled over to her. "Ms. Flick! You wanton trollop! Have you no sense of decency? There are innocent children in this neighborhood."

"You're lucky I'm not topless," she called back. "Not to mention, there isn't anyone innocent living around here."

I laughed. Ms. Flick was one of the few things I was going to miss when I left. "You're the kind of bad influence parents warn their kids about." I used my key to unlock our mailbox and rifled through the mail. Other than a bank statement for me, there was nothing but flyers and junk mail.

"Probably. There are few things scarier to some people than someone who's happy being exactly who she is. Just because the world thinks old ladies shouldn't flash a little skin doesn't mean I have to follow their rules."

"You never did strike me as much of a rule follower."

"Took me years to figure this out, so take advantage of my knowledge. It is far easier to make your own rules than it is to run around trying to follow everyone else's ideas of what you oughtta be doing." Ms. Flick wagged her finger in my direction. "Remember that when you're off at that fancy college in California. That, and don't let anyone tell you that you shouldn't wear a bikini."

I climbed the front steps. The screen door was hanging at a slight angle. "Any other advice?" I could do worse than listening to Ms. Flick.

She rubbed her chin and seemed to give the matter a lot of thought. "If you go out drinking, don't mix wine and hard liquor. If you start with the grape, stay with the grape. If you start with the grain, stay with the grain. Unless you want to spend the wee hours puking."

"I'll keep that in mind. I'll be around tomorrow if you still want to move your bookcases." Ms. Flick was widowed, so over the past few years I'd been helping her out with some of the heavier chores around her place. I planned to ask Brendan if he would check in on her once in a while when I was gone.

The inside of our trailer had to be at least thirty degrees hotter than outside. The aluminum siding seemed to absorb the sun's heat. My mom was lying on the sofa still in her uniform skirt from work, but she had stripped off her shirt and had just her bra on. Her bra was the sort of gray, dingy color that comes from being washed with black pants because doing two loads of laundry costs twice as much. She had a spray bottle filled with water in one hand that she dowsed herself with while the box fan propped on a crate beside the couch cooled her down. Yep, that was my family. Classy.

"How was work?" I asked, passing by the sofa to put the few things I'd picked up in the fridge. This is the benefit of living in a metal shoe box. It's small enough to have a conversation in opposite ends and still hear each other perfectly. I chucked the junk mail into the recycling box.

"We've got a convention in the hotel for the next couple of days, bunch of home-based makeup saleswomen." My mom was a maid at the Keppler. It used to be a destination for presidents and Hollywood stars way back when. Now most of the business came from conventions, weddings, and random rich people who liked to pretend they were presidents or Hollywood stars. The hotel had been built in the 1920s. I was pretty sure my mom felt like she had been cleaning rooms since then. It wasn't the kind of employment that was known for high levels of job satisfaction.

"I take it the makeup women are slobs?"

"Women are the worst. A woman traveling on her own is

just so glad she doesn't have to be the one cleaning that she'll go out of her way to let loose. They wipe their lipstick off on the towels, put their muddy shoes up on the bedspread, toss piles of empty wine bottles in the trash, and they don't even leave a dollar on the dresser when they're done. A man might be a slob, but his wife has trained him to know it, and he'll at least tip. Except for the real jerks."

"Huh." I turned to put the apples on the counter and slammed my hip against the sink. Stupid small kitchen. "What were you thinking about for dinner?"

Mom sighed. "It's too hot to make anything. Maybe we'll just have sandwiches."

When I was little, my mom had prided herself on being the übermom. She would have cookies waiting for me after school and would make all my Halloween costumes from scratch. I couldn't pinpoint the exact moment she'd decided she couldn't be bothered anymore, but it had been clear for some time that she had retired from the mom business. The most she was willing to do now was phone it in. "Sure. You want me to make them?"

"That would be great. Wait a bit though. I had a late lunch." My mom closed her eyes. She would lie there all night. In a while she would turn on the TV as background noise and spend the night reading one of her hundreds of romance novels. She would fall asleep with the book propped up on her chest and dream of a world full of swarthy pirates with hearts of gold and women whose dresses kept falling off.

I went to my room. Incoming college freshmen all over the world were wondering how they would ever fit everything they owned into a small dorm room. I, on the other hand, was thrilled with the idea of having more space. My twin bed and a dresser barely fit into the room. If the drawers were pulled out, they actually touched the bed. Years ago when I was in sort of a goth phase, I'd painted the walls a dark navy blue. I'd left them that way because it seemed like too much effort to paint over it. The dark paint didn't do much to make the space look any bigger. I flopped on the bed and looked up at the ceiling, bowed with age. I wondered if it was slowly going to press down on my head like a trash compactor. Maybe I should have gone out with Brendan. Sitting around here sweating and eating sandwiches made on day-old rolls my mom got from the hotel kitchen didn't exactly sound like a rocking good time.

I pulled the box of all my Berkeley stuff out from under my bed. My version of porn was pictures of college students wandering around various campuses. I couldn't get enough. I'd already memorized the college map for Berkeley and could tell you the exact distance from the Haviland building to the Calvin Laboratory. I'd gone online and toured every inch of the campus that was visible on Google Maps. I'd even ordered a sweatshirt with the giant University of California logo on the front. I would wear it all the time if I wouldn't sweat to death in this heat. For now, it was perfectly folded on top of my dresser in a place of honor. I could see it every time I walked in or out of the room.

I unfolded my acceptance letter. It was practically a holy relic as far as I was concerned. It was my official get-out-of-jail-free card. Ms. Lee, our school guidance counselor, had been annoyed with me. She kept pointing out that "given your family circumstances," I would have likely qualified for enough aid to get a free ride to one of the Seattle community colleges, or maybe even a university, as long as I was willing to stay in state. Ms. Lee wasn't a big believer in people like me dreaming big. I suspected she thought I would end up cleaning hotel rooms like my mom. She kept pointing out that going to Berkeley would mean having to pay out-of-state tuition and that my aid wouldn't cover all my costs. She kept stressing how challenging it would be. Maybe she thought a step up for me would be getting my hairdressing license and opening up some place on the island with a cheesy name like Kwick Klip or A Cut Above.

I never bothered to explain to Ms. Lee that the whole point of going to Berkeley was to get away. No one knew me in California. No one. I'd pulled a lot of cons over the past few years, but I was planning to pull the ultimate con starting in September. I was going to entirely remake my life. As far as anyone there would know, I grew up on a lovely resort island just off the coast of Seattle with a nice, normal family. I planned to leave off everything about my mom being a maid, us living in a trailer, my dad being in jail for another random "scheme" he had failed at, and the fact that I'd basically stolen the money to attend college. I was going to get a degree in architecture and travel the world designing beautiful buildings. No one was ever going to look down on me again.

I knew what I could do tonight. I'd go online and do some shopping for bedspreads. I'd exchanged a few e-mails with Cheryl, who was going to be my new roommate. The housing department had matched us up. So far I was pretty impressed. I'd been afraid I'd be matched with some bubbly cheerleader type who would clash with my preference for being cynical. It isn't that I don't like chronically happy people; I just see it as sort of a minor deformity, like having a cleft palate. Cheryl is from Oregon and is really into politics. She could list what legislation was currently being debated and tell you the name of the Speaker of the House. She sounded really serious about her education, and I could tell I wasn't going to have a problem with her swinging from the light fixtures while high on magic mushrooms. We were both going to be there to learn. She planned to change the world, and I planned to change my life. We'd talked about what each of us would bring in the fall and decided to buy new bedspreads so our beds would match.

I turned on my laptop so it would have time to warm up. It was ancient and practically the size of a briefcase. When I was done with it, I would have to donate it to a museum. That was one more thing I was going to have to get in the next couple weeks. I'd need something more up-to-date for college.

The list of stuff I needed to buy for school was huge. Brendan could laugh at my five-dollar cons if he wanted, but it had all added up. In three and a half weeks I would send the college my deposit, four thousand dollars. Then I figured it was going to be at least another five thousand to cover everything from the laptop, a decent suitcase, some new clothes, a new bedspread, and a plane ticket to San Fran. Right now the only suitcase I had was a beat-up duffel bag. If we traveled anywhere that required more stuff than could fit in there, my mom shoved it in garbage bags. Can you say tacky? As a joke, for graduation Brendan had given me a card announcing he'd gotten me a new set of luggage. When I opened the package, it was a box of Hefty trash bags. He'd pointed out that he'd sprung for the fancy bags with drawstrings. Ha ha ha.

I'd arranged a student loan and some grants to cover the rest of my tuition, but I knew I'd still need money for books and everything else during the year. Even if I got a part-time job, I was still going to go through my nest egg pretty quick. I pulled out the bank statement that had come in the mail and tore it open. I didn't need to read the statement; I could tell you exactly how much was in the account down to the penny, but seeing the figure in black and white made me relax. I'd been saving it for years, ever since I'd realized that if I wanted anything better than my current life, it was going to be up to me. And if I was going to go to the trouble of remaking my life, I didn't plan to settle for good enough. I was going to live in a dorm room with matching bedspreads and a roommate who would probably end up in Congress someday. I was going to get an amazing education and get a job that didn't involve cleaning toilets, or hoping not to get caught stealing. My life wasn't just going to be different; it was going to be *better*. It was worth every dollar I'd saved.

I looked down at the page and did a double take. I felt the blood fall out of my head. My ears started ringing, and it felt like I was going to either throw up or pass out, maybe both. I turned the page over in case something was written on the back. Nothing. I looked again in the envelope in case there was a note from the bank saying how they were just joking. Nothing.

The account balance read zero. All my money was gone. I was screwed.

chapter three

I practically flew out into the living room holding the bank statement above my head. Mom was rubbing her feet and watching a rerun of *Who Wants to Be a Millionaire* while rereading one of her historical romances. My mouth opened and closed, but I couldn't form any words. I wanted to demand we call the police. I wanted to scream I'd been robbed, but deep down I already knew the truth. I'd opened that account when I was a kid. I was too young then to have an account on my own; there was only one other name on it.

Mom sat up when she saw me. "Oh. I was going to talk to you about that."

"Tell me you didn't take my money." I held the statement in front of me like a shield.

"Your dad needed it. You know the court-appointed legal

assistance isn't worth a nickel. For your dad to stand a chance at early release, we need a halfway decent lawyer in his corner, and the lawyer needed more money to keep working. Then last week when we had that big rainstorm, I saw the roof was leaking again in the bathroom." Mom shrugged like she couldn't even remember all the various amounts of money she owed. "The bank wasn't going to lend me anything more."

"So you stole from me?" I screeched.

My mom stood up. "You need to calm down."

It felt like the top of my skull was going to blow off. "Calm down? Are you kidding? You took my college money."

"Sadie, I know you needed that money for school, but I needed that money for our family. Yes, school is important, but so is keeping a roof over our heads and getting your dad back. You keep talking about 'your' money, but you forget that we're a family, and that means we have to help each other out. You live here and I rarely ask you to chip in for costs."

I took a step back. I couldn't believe her. "You're my *mom*. It's not like you're doing me some big favor by letting me stay here. Sorry that you had me, and then you had to do all sorts of horrible things like feed me and provide me with basic housing and clothes." I motioned around the trailer. "And let me be sure to point out what a great job you've done, by the way, of providing me with everything my heart has ever dreamed about."

"Don't you *dare* imply I'm not doing everything I can," Mom snapped. "I work six days a week at that hotel."

"That money was my way out of here." I could hear the tears in my voice, and I swallowed them back down. "This was my chance to do better."

Mom walked into the kitchen, yanked out the rolls, and started to make sandwiches. She slathered the bread with generic-brand mayonnaise and deli ham. "Don't start. This isn't about you going to school. You could go to college in Seattle for free. This is about you going to some fancy school in California so you can feel important. You can still enroll in Seattle. You can live here and keep your job at the hotel on the weekends. If it still matters so much, then you can go away next year."

I looked around the room as if I expected someone to jump in and point out how twisted my mom's thinking was. "You can't be serious."

"You think you're the only one who wants better? *I* don't want to keep working at the hotel, and I've been there over twenty years. I don't want to live in this trailer either. I'm sorry your life hasn't been all sunshine, roses, and unicorns. Welcome to the real world, honey. This family needed that money and you're a part of this family. Sometimes you don't get what you want."

"You're acting like you did nothing wrong. You knew it was wrong or you would have asked me, but instead you just took it. You stole it."

Mom slapped the knife she had been using to spread mayonnaise down on the counter.

"You stole that money first, so get off your frickin' high horse."

I dropped the statement and stared at her.

She laughed when she saw my face. "What? You think I don't know what you and Brendan are up to all the time? You're a real chip off the block. Your dad should be proud."

"I'm nothing like him."

"Why, because you haven't got caught like he has? Maybe you're better at it than he is, but a con artist is a con artist. Your bluffing some rich boys out of a few dollars with a card trick isn't any better than your dad fencing hot car parts. You grew up with your dad; what else were you supposed to do? You lie down with dogs, you get up with fleas."

"I'm not like him," I said. She raised an eyebrow at me. "Yes, I pulled a few cons, but I did it because I needed money for school. There was a good reason for what I did."

"Even the devil has an excuse for doing wrong. You're not special there. The truth is, the villain of every story actually thinks he's the hero. Your dad has a good reason too. He takes care of this family. It's not like he's going to get some fancy job making big money. He does the best he can. We're all doing the best we can."

My entire body was shaking as if I was attached to a live wire. I was either going to melt down in full-on tears or start throwing things.

Mom sighed and rubbed her forehead. "Sadie, I'm sorry. I don't want to fight with you, and I don't think you're a bad kid. I wish we'd done better by you, but your dad and I have done our best. I promise, even though it might feel like it, your world isn't falling apart. This is a hurdle, and while I wish I could save you from every hard thing that is going to happen in your life, I can't. You're going to have to learn how to pick yourself up when the world knocks you down." She stepped out from behind the kitchen counter and took a step toward me, as if she was going in for a hug.

I stepped back quickly out of her reach. "The world didn't knock me down; you did. You're not trying to save me from a hurdle; you're throwing them out in front of me. I figured out early I'd better do whatever I had to, because no one in this family was going to help me." I yanked open the door. "And you know the biggest wrong of all, Mom? You apparently knew I was up to something all this time and you never even tried to stop me."

I slammed the screen door behind me and took off.

chapter four

The problem with living on an island is that you can't run away; you just end up running in circles.

I heard the ferry horn when I jumped onto my scooter and knew if I raced I had a chance to make it. I sprayed gravel from my back wheel as I came around the last corner. The ferry worker saw me coming and held the gate, giving me a chance to pull onto the ferry car deck.

"Cutting it close," he said, snapping the chain behind me. He pushed the red button that told the captain the boat was loaded and ready to go. The horn blew again, the sound bouncing off the water. Most people stayed in their cars for the short, twenty-minute crossing, but the car deck always smelled like stale gasoline to me, and not being able to see the horizon made me nauseated. I usually stood at the front, letting the wind blow my hair into a giant, knotted beehive, but today there was a group of kids from my high school there. Everyone was dressed up, so they must have been headed over to the clubs. Susan Warren was wearing high heels that had to be at least six inches high. She was going to regret that plan in a few hours, and unless she had magical abilities, there was no way a pair of comfortable shoes could be crammed into her paperback-book-size silver purse.

I climbed the metal stairs up to the passenger lounge. "Lounge" might be a bit fancy for what it really was: a few rows of plastic benches, a bathroom that was always out of order, and a row of vending machines. It was a small metal cell crammed between the ferry bridge and the car deck. I sat in the first row with my back pressed against the wall so that I could look out the windows. I could see the lights of the city, with the Space Needle lit up. Unlike the island, where to feel alone I had to find an isolated spot, I tended to feel alone in Seattle by being in a crowd. The ferry would dock just a couple of blocks from Pike Place Market. It would be closed by now, but I could walk down to Pioneer Square and perch in a coffee shop for a few hours. Maybe seeing normal people would make me feel more normal. I stuffed my hands in my pockets and felt the change from the grocery store. Turns out, this was all the money I had in the world now.

I couldn't believe my mom had compared me to my dad. He and I were never close. I suppose it's hard to bond with a parental figure when he's in prison for most of those important formative years. I flashed on second grade, when Burke Huntington had teased me for saying my dad was at camp.

"Grown-ups don't go to camp, stupid." Burke had laughed with his beaklike nose in the air. "Your dad is in jail!" The other kids crowded around the swings laughed too, and in that instant I knew he was right and I felt crushing hot shame. I ran out of the playground and down the five blocks from the school to the hotel. The front desk clerk called my mom when I burst into the lobby crying, with snot running down my chin.

My mom had hustled me out of the hotel lobby before the manager could spot me and get her into trouble. Guests at the Keppler paid far too much per night to be disturbed by unpleasantness. She steered me into the giant industrial kitchen and bent down to talk to me behind the racks of clean, pressed tablecloths. Puffs of steam from the giant pots on the row of stoves hung in the room like fog, and there was a constant clatter of knives coming from the line of prep cooks. I had managed to spit out what had happened in between gasping, hiccuping sobs.

"What made you say he was at camp?" Mom smelled like the industrial lemon cleaner they used.

I shrugged. I thought about all the visits to my dad, sitting on the picnic tables out in the yard. He and all the other guys wore gray uniforms with orange reflector strips along the sleeves and pant legs. My dad always had something he'd made for my mom, a crocheted afghan, a wooden plaque with her name in cursive letters burned across the top. They'd never told me he was in camp; it must have been something I'd just assumed. Burke was right. I was stupid. I shrugged and buried my face in my mom's shoulder. She called the school and told them I was sick. She had one of the chefs make me a grilled cheese sandwich. I spent the afternoon in the laundry room, squishing myself between the backs of washers and dryers, waiting for her to finish her shift, surrounded by the smell of clean sheets and towels. The other maids had stopped by every so often to check on me. They told me goofy knock-knock jokes and slipped me candy. I had stuffed myself with the chocolates that were supposed to lie on the guests' pillows until I'd felt like throwing up.

Even when my dad wasn't in jail, we weren't particularly close. It was obvious he was crazy about my mom, but I always had the sense that he was looking at me from the corner of his eye as if he wasn't quite sure what I was doing there. It was like he was somewhat surprised to see me. I felt like a houseguest who had long outstayed her welcome whenever he was around. A few years ago my dad had busted in on me in my room making out with some boy I'd met on the beach. My top was off and the berry lip gloss I'd been wearing was smeared down my chin. The boy had jumped up, no doubt panicked that an enraged father was about to pulverize him, but instead my dad had backed out of my room looking as if he had discovered a nest of roaches. He never mentioned it again. No heart-to-heart talk about how I should value myself and my body. No warnings about getting pregnant and ruining my life, or even a lecture about how he expected more of me. It was like he couldn't be bothered.

If I ever took the time to talk to our school counselor, Ms. Lee, about my actual feelings, instead of avoiding her whenever possible, she would no doubt tell me that my tendency to pull cons was a plea for attention. I was a pathetic psych textbook example of a girl who didn't get enough attention from her daddy. If there were any decent guys to choose from on the island, I would probably be a slut, trying to spread my legs into feeling loved. I might not have a lot else going for me, but I had enough self-respect not to sleep with the guys on the island. Except for Brendan. Although I was willing to admit that had been a huge mistake, at least he wasn't an asshole.

The horn blared, indicating we were about to dock. I slid off the bench and headed for the stairs. I paused, looking at the wall of notices stuck to the bulletin board. A Volkswagen Bug for sale. Babysitting services—References available! Piano lessons. I looked closer at a flyer advertising puppies for sale. Westies. I ran my finger along the phone number. I would love to have a dog. I even had a name picked out: Lloyd, after Frank Lloyd Wright. Someday.

I was about to walk back downstairs to get my scooter when I saw a photo of myself on the board. MISSING was printed in bright red letters across the top. There was a photo of a little girl directly below the photo of me. That's when I realized it wasn't me. It was one of those age-enhanced Photoshopped pictures.

There was a note that this might be what Ava, the little girl, would look like now, fifteen years after she'd gone missing. I backed up and squinted at the two pictures. I suspected if poor Ava had been missing for fifteen years, she looked a lot more like a corpse than like the aged photo. I'd watched enough *Dateline* to know missing kids didn't usually come to a happy ending. It was weird how much the aged photo looked like me . . . or *would* look like me if I didn't dye my hair. I couldn't decide if it was neat or kinda creepy.

The ferry horn gave another blast, rattling the cheap plastic chairs. We'd be disembarking in minutes. I had to get downstairs so people wouldn't be stuck behind my parked scooter. I started to walk away, but on sudden impulse I turned back. I tore the flyer off the board and stuffed it into my pocket. I wasn't sure what I was going to do with it, but I wanted it.

chapter five

I parked my scooter in the free lot near the ferry dock. I had the change from the grocery, but that wasn't going to get me very far. I needed money, and this wasn't the time to go straight and get a second part-time job. I ducked into a 7-Eleven that smelled like boiled hot dogs and used the money I had to buy twelve Hershey's bars.

I didn't have time to do things right. I usually printed up paper bands that I could wrap around the chocolate bars to make them look more official, but I was going to have to work with what I had tonight. I ducked into the bathroom and made sure my hair looked good and that I didn't have mascara smeared under my eyes from crying. Looking wholesome was critical to my plan.

Armed with the candy bars, I stepped back outside and looked over my options. The Four Seasons Hotel was nearby.

As I drew closer, I knew I'd hit the jackpot. There was a group of businesspeople in the lobby, a sea of gray and black suits. Perfect. I plastered a smile on my face and headed toward a cluster of men while keeping an eye out for any hotel employees.

"Hello!" I gave them a small wave. "My name is Molly, and I'm a member of the debate team at West Seattle High." I'd found with the business crowd, debate was the best draw. Among an arty crowd, I pretended to be either with the band or in the performing arts. At a sports bar, I went with being either a cheerleader or on the girl's basketball team. The trick to any good con is to know your audience.

"We're trying to raise money to go to state competitions in the fall. Would you consider buying a chocolate bar to help us out?" I held out one bar to the group of suits with another of my perky, future corporate leader of America smiles.

One guy was already pulling out his wallet. "Can't argue with teaching kids critical thinking. Unless they're my kids, of course. I could use a little less debate at home." Everyone laughed, and I joined in like I thought he was stand-up comic kind of funny. "How much?"

"The candy bars are five dollars," I said.

"All right, give me two."

I passed him two of the candy bars, which had cost me far less than five bucks, with a smile and pocketed the profit. Two others bought one each, and I moved on to the next group. I managed to sell another five before the front desk clerk seemed to start tracking my movements. I left the hotel before she could have one of the bell staff approach me.

I got lucky. Right across the street from the hotel there were a group of college kids outside a bar. I jaywalked over to them and shared how I was trying to raise money for our school to host a battle of the bands competition. I was able to sell the rest of my candy bars in less than five minutes.

It was starting to rain. I ducked into a Starbucks. I ordered a medium black coffee in a large cup and then poured milk in up to the top, the cheap woman's latte. I folded myself into one of the large, worn wingback chairs sprinkled around the room. I grabbed a section of the paper from the rack and opened it on my lap to advertise I was busy and wasn't interested in chatting up any strangers.

I did the math quickly in my head. The candy bars had cost me just under fifteen dollars and I'd sold them for sixty, clearing forty-five dollars in less than thirty minutes. It was better money than I made working as a waitress at the hotel, but I was going to have to sell cases of candy bars if I was going to come up with the thousands I needed to send Berkeley for my deposit by August first. I bit my lip to keep from crying again. I forced myself to take a deep breath. I wasn't prepared to roll over and give up.

In theory, my mom was right. I could take classes at one of the community colleges in Seattle or try getting into the University of Washington. The hotel would keep me on for work. If the restaurant was slow, then the cleaning crew could always use another maid.

Between working at the hotel and pulling some extra cons here and there, I would be able to squirrel away enough money to go the following year. I could worry about what I would need for the rest of my time there once I was in. Berkeley would likely let me delay my admission a year with no trouble.

Logic said waiting a year was an option, but my heart started to beat faster when I thought about it. I knew that if I didn't go now, I would never go. One year would become two, and then three. Then I'd be offered shift supervisor in the restaurant, which would mean extra money, so I'd tell myself how I would go back to school the next term, but I wouldn't. I'd end up marrying Brendan, because after all, he was there and asking and who was I to be so picky? We'd have a couple of kids who would be teased in school for not having any money the same way we were, and Brendan and I would fight over stupid things like who drank the last of the milk or how to pay for car repairs, and the big event in our lives would be if we decided to upgrade our cable package. I'd be one of those people who talked about all the things I was going to do someday, all while everyone around me didn't bother listening because they knew I wouldn't.

I pulled the MISSING flyer out of my pocket and smoothed out the wrinkles. I took time to read the whole thing this time.

MISSING

Ava McKenna (age 3) went missing fifteen years ago on July 30 from the Keppler Hotel. A photo of how

she may look now is below. A reward of $250,000 is offered for any information leading to her recovery.

A phone number and website were listed on the bottom of the sheet. Two hundred and fifty thousand dollars. My mind started to spin. Was there a way to use the fact that I looked like the photo? I didn't look exactly like the picture, but I was close, and with a bit of a makeover I could look even closer. I didn't need the whole quarter of a million; I'd settle for ten thousand of it. All I needed to do was find the missing Ava.

Or convince them I was Ava.

chapter six

I took the last ferry home after having stayed in the coffee shop until it closed and they basically kicked me out. I slipped into my room without talking to my mom. I'd seen the sliver of light under her door when I came in, but I didn't want to talk to her. I'd completely forgotten I was scheduled to work the next day until my alarm went off.

I preferred to work the main hotel restaurant called the Palms, but today I was stuck in the banquet hall. There was a lunch buffet for the women attending the makeup sales convention.

The point of a buffet is people are supposed to eat the food that is provided on the buffet. It isn't a complex concept. However, it was clear the makeup ladies were not familiar with this radical dining idea. They would pull me over to the table and ask if they could get a sandwich without any mayo? Could I be a dear and check in the back to see if there was a raspberry vinaigrette for the salad? They didn't care for the dressing that was on the buffet. Could someone bring them a small bowl of that fabulous clam chowder they had yesterday with dinner? I managed to avoid tossing soup at anyone, or screaming that I wasn't getting tipped so they could stick their no-mayo sandwich where the sun didn't shine.

I could tell my hair was starting to frizz, because there were pieces that had escaped the regulation bun and were stuck to my sweating forehead. I had soup spilled on my black pants and a splash of the requested raspberry vinaigrette on my shirt. Waiting tables was not a glamorous job. I was struggling to carry a full coffee urn to the coffee station in the corner of the banquet hall when someone reached around me and took it from my hands. Brendan smiled and winked.

"So, are you going to take out the empty one, or do you want me to stand here holding this all day?"

His voice jolted me out of my surprise. "What are you doing here?" I looked around to make sure no one had noticed him. I yanked the empty urn out of the holder so Brendan could put the full one in its place. He hefted it into the holder as if it weighed nothing.

"Most people would just say thank you," Brendan said. "I'm here because you left me a bunch of messages last night saying you wanted me."

I rolled my eyes. "I didn't say anything about wanting you. I said I wanted to talk, and I only left one message."

"You made at least two other calls. I saw your number come up." Brendan backed up so one of the ladies could reach the coffee urn. "Here, allow me." He poured a cup and passed it gallantly to her. She took it, flushing, her other hand fiddling with her pearls.

I waited until she walked away. "If you saw my number, why didn't you pick up?"

"You know what they say: Absence makes the heart grow fonder." He ran his finger gently down the side of my face. I whacked it away.

"You're going to get me in trouble."

Brendan laughed. Being in trouble was a natural state to him. "So what? You're going to quit in a few weeks anyway. Why not go out with a bang? How about I throw you up on the dessert table and we go at it in front of this crowd? I bet these ladies have a freaky side." Brendan took a step closer, as if he were about to hoist me up on top of the cheesecake slices.

"I might not be quitting. That's what I need to talk to you about."

Brendan's face dropped the smirk. "Is everything okay?"

I caught the eye of Mr. Stein, the banquet manager. He was standing in the doorway to the kitchen. "Shit. I have to go. I'm off in an hour. Meet me at the cove?"

"Of course." Brendan grabbed my elbow before I walked away. "I would have called back right away if I knew you needed me. You know that, right?"

"I know." I grabbed the empty urn and headed back to the kitchen before Mr. Stein was motivated to give me his standard lecture on the importance of having a good work ethic, and that he didn't get promoted to manager by chitchatting with his friends while on the clock.

Brendan could frustrate me faster than any person alive, but I never doubted for a minute that he would be there for me. I couldn't remember a time when he wasn't in my life. Our dads had met in jail. Now, there was a charming story we could tell the grandkids if we ever married. Brendan had been my friend since we were toddlers, which is why I never should have slept with him.

Brendan had many challenges in his life, but the two advantages he had in his favor were that he was tremendously good-looking and that he obviously had that whole "bad boy" charm going for him. He wasn't shy about using either of these to get what he wanted. By eleventh grade he'd slept with not only every girl in our class, but also most of the summer girls who visited the hotel. It was the combination of his dark curly hair, which he let grow a bit wild, his half smile that showed his chipped front tooth, and his ability to smooth talk anyone with the sound of his voice that worked like magic.

I was most likely the only one who didn't sleep with him because of his charm. I slept with him because he could make me laugh, and because I didn't want to go to college as a virgin. I didn't want to be a virgin, but I wasn't desperate enough to sleep with anyone else in our class or some random summer guest. They say the first time is fairly dismal, so it made sense to get it over with someone I liked, and I wouldn't look back on with horror. Plus, there was the advantage that with all his practice, Brendan would know what he was doing. What had surprised me was that Brendan didn't immediately agree. I'd had to talk him into the plan.

Brendan had insisted that if we were going to do it, it had to be somewhere special. Of course, given the state of our finances, it had to be somewhere special on a budget. We'd gone camping up in the woods. Brendan had decked out the tent with a lantern and loads of quilts and blankets so we wouldn't freeze. It was early May, but it was still too cold to be sleeping outside. He'd packed a picnic for us and insisted that we have dinner before starting.

"So should I take my clothes off?" I'd motioned to my T-shirt. "I brought condoms too, in case you didn't have any."

"Where's the romance?" Brendan had asked, wiping the last of the red velvet cake from his mouth.

I'd rolled my eyes at him. "Aren't you the one who says romance is the ultimate con?" I poked him in the stomach. "You don't have to pretend with me. I've already agreed to sleep with you. Heck, I'm the one who asked you. Think of it as a favor for a friend. And if you want romance, condoms scream romance. It's the gift that says, 'I care enough to make sure you don't get some kind of disease or end up knocked up.' See? I've got both your practical and romantic sides covered."

Brendan had shifted uncomfortably. "Are you sure you want to do this? The first time is sort of a big deal."

"Can you even remember the name of the first girl you slept with?" I'd asked. I was getting nervous the more we talked about it.

"It's different for girls," Brendan had said.

"Maybe for some girls. I've never been the type to write my name in a heart with a guy's. I don't save flowers from dances or any of that overemotional stuff. This is something I just want to get over with. It's bad enough I'm the last virgin in our class. I don't plan to be the only one at college."

"You're not the last virgin in our class."

"Yes, let's not forget there's also Tina, who weighs at least three hundred pounds, and Derek, who wears that T-shirt about Jesus being his best friend. Great company I'm in."

"Lots of people stay virgins. You don't need to worry about what other people think or are doing. You're not as tough and cynical as you want people to believe, you know."

"You're not going to turn all Dr. Phil on me, are you?" I leaned back against a pile of quilts.

"I just think it should be something special." Brendan shrugged.

"You realize how that sounds coming out of your mouth, right?" I'd sighed and rolled over so I could crawl out of the tent. "Forget it. If you don't want to do it, we won't."

"What, you're going to find someone else?"

"No, Brendan, if you won't sleep with me, then I intend to

save myself until marriage. Or perhaps I'll join a nunnery instead and give up the idea of sex altogether."

I moved closer to the door flap. The whole plan was stupid. I suddenly felt embarrassed, and I wanted to get out of there. Brendan grabbed my wrist before I could leave. He pulled me back and kissed me deeply.

I pulled back, my breath coming faster. "You don't have to do this."

"Come here." Brendan had pulled me closer. "If we're going to do this, then it will be something you never forget."

He was right about that. We'd slept together months ago, and every day since then it was there between us. I'd thought my virginity was something that I wanted to ditch, like getting rid of an unwanted, ugly sofa in the living room. I saw it as something that I was practically willing to pay someone to cart away, but it had turned into something else. That night had changed things between us. We'd been friends forever, but now it was different. The moment I woke up in the tent, curled up with him, I knew it had been a mistake. I hadn't expected to feel anything, and even more importantly, I didn't want to. There was nowhere for our relationship to go. I was leaving and Brendan was staying. It was just one more thing in my life that was a dead end.

chapter seven

Keeper's Cove was on the west side of the island. There wasn't a beach, just black rocks crusted with purple starfish and clumps of mussels at low tide leading into the water. Without a sandy beach it didn't attract tourists. There was no place to lie out in a three-hundred-dollar swimsuit that shouldn't be exposed to salt water. The only living creatures I ever saw out at the cove were the otters, who liked to lie in the sunshine on the rocks, and Mr. Chin, who liked to come out after a big storm looking for glass Japanese floaters that may have washed up onto the shore.

I pulled off my shoes and socks and scrambled down the rocks to the water. Brendan was standing at the edge, skipping stones over the waves. His shirt was off and I could see the muscles in his back. I wanted to kick myself for noticing. I never used to pay attention to how he looked. I stopped to roll up the cuffs of the black dress pants I'd worn to work. I'd already peeled off my white blouse, leaving only the white tank top I had on underneath. I wished I had thought to bring something to change into after work. I hated that he looked good while I looked sweaty and smelled like kitchen grease.

Brendan crouched down and pulled two cans of Diet Coke out of the cold water. He held one out to me.

"Wow. If you'd brought food, you'd have thought of everything," I said.

"Oh, ye of little faith, of course I thought of everything." Brendan pulled a Kit Kat bar out of his pocket and tossed it over. "Now, what's up?"

I opened the can and sat down on a rock. I put my feet in the water and hissed. The water was so cold that it felt hot at first, but then my feet went slightly numb. It felt good after running all afternoon around the banquet hall. I took a deep breath. I wondered if saying the truth aloud would make it any better than the way I remembered it. "My mom took all my college money. All of it. She said she needed it for bills and my dad's lawyer, and that was more important than what I wanted."

Brendan whistled and sat down next to me. I could feel the heat from his skin. "You must have freaked out."

"Understatement." I snapped off part of the Kit Kat and offered it to Brendan. "If I don't come up with a minimum of four grand by August first, I'm going to lose my place at Berkeley. So much for getting out of here."

Brendan was quiet and we watched the waves. About fifteen feet from shore, a fish jumped out of the water, its silver scales flashing in the light before it dropped back in. I wondered if it was trying to escape the ocean. Most likely it was about to be eaten by something larger than it.

Brendan tossed a rock into the water. "You know you can still sign up at one of the community colleges. Heck, maybe it'll even motivate me to take a class or two if I know you'll be there to watch out for me."

I felt a flash of anger. Everyone seemed to think I should settle. "I'm *not* going to community college."

"So you've got a plan to come up with four large?"

My anger evaporated. "That's why I called you. I need your help."

"I've got maybe a couple hundred I can lend you. I could try hocking my stereo in Seattle, but I'm not sure it's going to bring in much. Those places always rip you off."

I touched his arm. "I didn't mean I want your money. I have an idea. If there's a way to pull it off, then there will be plenty of money."

Brendan raised an eyebrow. I pulled the MISSING poster out of my pocket, unfolding it before passing it over. I found myself holding my breath. Maybe my resemblance to the age-enhanced photo wasn't that great and the whole plan was a bust. Not that I had much of a plan at this point.

Brendan looked down at the poster with his eyebrows drawn

together for a second and then a smile spread across his face. He looked up at me, then back down at the poster. "Well, look at that. If you aren't a long-lost missing heiress."

"You think it looks like me too?" I felt a rush of relief.

Brendan held up the poster. "The nose isn't quite right, but I would say it's pretty close. If you did your hair different, you would be a ringer. You could work an angle on this for sure. It's not like this age-enhancing stuff is an exact science."

I fidgeted on the rock. "Did you see the reward amount?"

"Quarter of a million is a bit of a jump from your usual five-dollar con limit," Brendan pointed out.

"I can't figure out how to pull it off though. If I come forward and announce I'm the mysterious missing Ava, I'm betting Mom and Dad McKenna are going to want to do a DNA test, and that's the end of that plan."

"Even if we found a way around the DNA test, it's more than that. This kid has been missing for fifteen years. You suddenly showing up, the sorry little rich girl found at last, is going to be a big deal. We're talking CNN, *People* magazine, movie-of-the-week kind of big deal. Whatever cover story you've come up with is going to be under huge scrutiny. Everyone we went to school with is going to be interviewed. It'll be a lot of pressure and attention."

I cut him off. "I know." I chucked a rock in the water. It sank without skipping even once. "Then there's the fact that if I say I'm the missing Ava, my parents are basically guilty of kidnapping, and I'm pretty sure that guarantees them both a one-way ticket to prison." I shrugged. "Of course, my dad is already there, so at least for him it's a short trip."

"On the upside, you're pissed at your mom already. It's a win-win in that way. You pull off the con, and you get her back for taking your cash."

"Now that I think about it, the whole idea was stupid." I rubbed my palms on my pants. "I don't know why I told you. I guess I thought maybe you would see a way around all of this." I went to grab the poster back from Brendan, but he held it out of my reach.

"You're going at this the wrong way. No way a straight approach will work. Too many things that could go wrong, too much attention. The more people looking, the more likely someone is going to see what you don't want them to. You don't need two hundred and fifty thousand, so don't go after that." Brendan wasn't looking at me, he was staring out at the ocean. I could practically see the gears in his brain working.

"So what do I do?"

Brendan smiled. "You've been thinking backward. You're looking for someone to give you money because Ava's been found. What you need to do is figure out how much is it worth to someone to keep Ava missing."

chapter eight

My dad always says the snake in the garden was the first con artist in history, sweet-talking Eve into taking a bite of the apple for his own gain. He says a profession as old and established as grafting should be treated with more respect. Then again, my dad is currently finishing off a two-year sentence for bilking people out of their money in a real estate pyramid scheme, so take his advice for what it's worth.

There are as many cons as there are con artists, from bar bets to street hustles, carnival scams, card tricks, and Internet fraud. For the con to work, you need the mark, or the victim, to be naive, greedy, fearful, or insecure. Cons always point out that you can't cheat an honest man.

I turned over Brendan's plan. The idea of taking money from people looking for their lost daughter still missing after fifteen years hadn't sat very well with me, even with Berkeley on the line. I'd never pulled a con based on someone else's fear before. It might sound twisted, but while I knew what I did was unethical and wrong, there was a limit to how wrong I was willing to be. My dad worked a con for several years where he pretended to be a psychic. For a price, he would connect people with the ghosts of their long-lost loved ones. He argued that it made people feel better. They had a chance to resolve things, maybe say "I love you" one more time. To me it felt slimy. I felt better than him because I'd convinced myself my cons never really hurt anyone. You might pay more for a candy bar than you should, but in the end, you were still supporting a charity, just not the one you thought.

"How much do you know about the McKenna family?" Brendan asked.

I paused to think about it. "Well, their names are in the news a lot. They donated a million dollars or something to the Seattle Children's Hospital recently. He runs an architecture firm in Seattle. They recently designed a new museum in California that won a whole bunch of awards."

"Aw, isn't that cute, you have something in common other than looking like his long-lost daughter." Brendan laughed and I jabbed him in the side to make him stop. I had a thing for buildings. Some girls loved shoes and handbags, but for me it was architecture. I dreamed of designing houses. Not cookie-cutter McMansions either. My houses were going to be environmentally friendly, and I planned to design them for people who wanted a real home, not a giant extension of their ego and proof of their bank account.

"I don't think our mutual love of building design means he's going to fork over a few grand so I can go to college," I pointed out.

"Do they have any other kids?"

"I don't think so, but I'm not sure." I searched my memory. "I don't remember ever hearing anything about any kids, but it could mean that they just keep them out of the limelight."

"That's the first thing to check. If there is another sibling around, the last thing they're going to want is to have Ava show back up on the scene. It'll mean dividing Mommy and Daddy's attention now, and a big fat inheritance later."

"That's a cold way to think of it."

"Cold but true. You need to start thinking of who has something to gain by keeping missing Ava out of the picture. You've got some research ahead of you. You need to learn everything you can about the disappearance, about the family, hell, about anything that might end up being something we could use. Information is power. The more we know, the more likely we'll be able to figure out an angle on the whole thing."

I stood up and brushed off my pants. "It looks like I've got a date with my laptop. I'll call you if I find anything."

"Call me either way. I might see something that you don't."

I watched the waves as they came into shore. "Thanks for

helping. I know you don't want me to go away to school. I appreciate you helping me anyway."

"Yeah, well, that's me, all-around great guy. Of course, it could be that I just like the idea of you owing me a big favor. Never know when that might come in handy." Brendan gave a fake evil laugh and stood.

I laughed for real. "Great, this means I'm going to end up mixed up in one of your schemes, doesn't it?"

"That's not the kind of favor I had in mind," Brendan said, staring into my eyes. I felt pinned in place. Even though we were outside, I suddenly felt claustrophobic, as if he had backed me into a corner.

I shifted nervously. "Sounds like trouble," I said, taking a step back. I looked at my arm as if I were wearing a watch warning me of the time. "I should head home and start on all this research."

Brendan stepped closer and lightly touched the side of my face. "Why do you keep running away from me?"

"I'm not running," I said. "I just want to get home and get out of these clothes. You know how black polyester pants give me hives."

Brendan's eyes narrowed. He knew a lame joke when he heard it. "You can try lying to me, but don't lie to yourself. You're avoiding me. You have been for months. You never want to do anything anymore. Every time I call, you're busy. You think I don't notice?"

"I've been busy. There were finals to get through, and then everything with graduation. I've been picking up extra shifts at the hotel whenever I can because I need the money. Then there are things with my mom; she's been all weirded out about the idea of me leaving, especially with my dad being locked up. I don't think she likes the idea of being on her own." I paused to take a deep breath and realized I was rambling. "Besides, I still see you."

"If you're not avoiding me, then let's go out."

"I can't go out. I'm dressed for work. I smell. I'm tired from running around all day."

"Fine, let's go tomorrow."

I sighed. I was boxed in. "Look, it's awkward."

"What? Because we made love?"

I cringed. I hated the term "made love." It sounded like one of my mom's cheesy romance novels. Like any minute he might start talking about his loins being on fire. Why couldn't he say "had sex" like everyone else, or better yet, why couldn't he not bring it up at all? "Yes, it's awkward because we slept together," I admitted.

"Look, I know I have a reputation, but this is different. I would never hurt you," Brendan said.

I wanted to scream. "Yes, but I would. I'd hurt *you*; it seems like I already have. I don't want to see you because I feel guilty. I can't be in a relationship with you. Sleeping together was a mistake. I thought it wouldn't change things, but it did. You're my friend, most likely the best friend I ever had or will ever have, but we can't date."

"Why?" Brendan's face flushed. He was angry. "Doesn't it seem like that is the best place for a relationship to start? With being friends? I'm not saying we should go grab some rings and get married; I'm saying we should go on a few dates, see where things go."

"I don't need to see where things are going. I *know* where they're going! I'm going to college. I'm going away. There isn't a future in this, with us. We shouldn't have had sex. I thought it could be, just, I don't know, a friends with benefits kind of thing, but it's clear you want more. Only I can't give you more."

"I want more?" Brendan laughed. "Oh, that's rich. Are you saying you felt nothing? I was there, remember?" He yanked me close and kissed me, my mouth opening under his. I could feel the burn of his stubble as his face pressed down on mine. I could feel the heat coming off his body through my clothing. I tried to pull away, but he held me closer for a second before letting go. "Call me crazy, but it feels like you want more too. Maybe you don't want to admit it, but you do," he said.

Brendan stomped past me and clambered up the rocks, back to his car. My fingers touched my lips. I could see my hand was shaking slightly. I couldn't tell what I was upset about . . . that Brendan had kissed me or that he'd stopped?

chapter nine

I took a sip of my Diet Coke. It had gone flat and warm. I stretched my head to one side and then the other to get the kink out of my neck. I'd spent the past few hours on the computer. I had stacks of notes spread all over the bed. Being a good con artist isn't all based on charm; research is required. I now knew a bunch of facts about the McKenna family.

The McKenna family had money dating back to the eighteen hundreds, when Mr. McKenna's great-great-grandfather had been a lumber baron. Their house in Seattle's Montlake area looked from the photos to be roughly the size of a castle. Our entire trailer would have fit on the front porch. Not that they would let us park our rusted trailer anywhere near their contemporary mansion.

Fifteen years ago they came to Bowton Island for a vacation.

They stayed at the Keppler Hotel. On the third day of their vacation, while Mr. and Mrs. McKenna were out sailing with friends, their three-year-old daughter, Ava, went missing while being watched by the nanny. The McKennas hired private investigators, and huge amounts of reward money were offered, but nothing ever showed up. Not Ava, not her body, not a ransom demand. It was like Ava had simply disappeared.

I'd found hundreds of articles that came out around the time Ava went missing, but there was more recent stuff too, the occasional human interest story, a plea for any new leads because the case remained open. A few years ago some bones were found on the island, and for a brief period of time people thought it might be Ava's body, but it turned out to be the ribs of a dog.

Some good came out of the tragedy. Mrs. McKenna found her mission in life after her daughter went missing. She started a nonprofit group, the McKenna Children's Foundation. It spent millions on helping families with missing kids and on providing less privileged kids access to early education.

Mrs. McKenna wasn't the only one who found her calling after Ava disappeared. Their nanny was Nancy Goodall. I'd seen her on TV a bunch of times. She'd started a security company that specialized in children. She marketed her guilt—"I failed a child, but you don't have to fail yours"—into a security gold mine. The company sold nanny cams, kits where you could collect your kids' DNA and fingerprints in case they ever went missing, stuff like that. She tended to show up on TV whenever a kid went missing, lecturing on what families could do to keep this from happening to their children. She was a regular on CNN and the talk-show circuit. She had recently started her own cable show. I could hardly wait to miss it.

I looked down at all my notes. I'd written down all the details I thought might be important. I flipped through the pages to see if anything jumped out. The whole thing made me sad. The idea of just not knowing what happened must have eaten Ava's parents alive. I imagined that at first they prayed she was okay, but eventually they must have just wished to find her body, something to put the whole thing to rest. I had a mental image of Mrs. McKenna walking through Pacific Place shopping mall in Seattle, looking at the face of every teen girl she saw and wondering if it might be her daughter.

I pulled out a bunch of our family photos. I wanted to see how I looked compared to Ava at age three. I found all my old school photos. There was a tragic goth phase in freshman year, when I had worn so much eyeliner it's a wonder I didn't develop some sort of allergy. I couldn't find any pictures of me before age four. In the photos of me at four, my hair was cut so short I looked like some sort of prison inmate. I'd picked through the rest of the photos in the shoe box, but while I'd found a few pictures of my parents from when they first got married, there were no baby pictures. This is what happens when you keep your family mementos in a couple of beat-up old shoe boxes. We weren't the kind of family that did a lot of scrapbooking. Construction paper, glitter pens, and happy-face stickers were in short supply at our place.

"What are you working on? School's over; you should be free from homework." I jumped. Mom was leaning against the doorjamb. I hadn't even heard her come in. She was still wearing her maid uniform from the hotel. There were dark circles under her eyes, and her makeup had worn off during the day until all that was left was a trace of her berry pink lipstick bleeding into the lines around her mouth.

"This? This is nothing, just something I wanted to check out." I quickly shuffled all the papers into a pile before she could see them.

Her eyebrow went up slightly. "Doesn't look like nothing."

"I'm checking into student loans and grants." I crossed my arms over my chest, daring her to ask me more.

Her eyes shifted away. "Any luck?"

I shrugged and waited to see if she would say sorry for taking the money.

"I brought home a pizza. No green peppers, double mushrooms," she said. Ordering my favorite pizza was as close as I was going to get to an apology.

I followed her into the living room and plunked down on the sofa. I grabbed a slice out of the box. Mom picked a few of the mushrooms off. She wasn't a 'shroom lover like me.

"Your dad called this morning. He was disappointed he missed you." She nibbled on her pizza. "You weren't home when he called last time either."

Ah, the pizza came with extra mushrooms and a side of guilt. "I had to work."

"You know he can't just call whenever he likes. He's only allowed to use the phone at set times."

"I think that's the point of jail, the whole restriction-of-freedom thing," I said. Next my mom would be pointing out that prison officials were cruel because my dad wasn't allowed to wander home whenever he wanted.

"You don't need to be such a brat." Mom waved her pizza in my direction. "You know why they don't send donkeys to college?"

"No one likes a smart-ass," I answered. This was a very old joke in our house.

"The point I'm making is that your dad misses you."

"I'm not avoiding his calls; I had to work." This wasn't completely true. My dad and I tended to avoid each other. It was a mutual thing. I always felt that he'd never wanted kids; he always looked at me as if he was wondering when I might leave. He was never the kind of dad who got down on his hands and knees and played with me as a kid when he was even around, and as I got older, we seemed to have even less to talk about. My mom, however, liked to have this fantasy where we were the perfect family. I'm pretty sure inside her mind we had a nice cozy bungalow with a white picket fence and a golden Lab named Buster.

When she talked about our lives, I almost didn't recognize them. She had this ability to completely remake history to fit her fantasy. She would talk about how when I starred in the school play in eighth grade, my dad brought me flowers after the show. I'm not sure where she got that idea; he hadn't even shown up to the play, and I wasn't the star; I was some background player. All her family memories where straight out of a Hallmark card, with us wearing matching holiday sweaters while we made Christmas cookies together. For years I thought I was going crazy, since I didn't remember all these things, but then I realized she just made them up. Cut out any parts of her life she didn't like and squished in a new and better memory to fill the gap.

"Your dad thinks he might be released early. They've got overcrowding issues, and he doesn't have any disciplinary reports this time. The lawyer is pulling together something to take to the probation board."

"Dad always did master the good behavior part on the inside. It's when he's released that he has a problem." I saw Mom open her mouth to argue with me, and I held up my hand to stop her. "I'm joking."

"I was thinking when he gets out, we could still take a summer vacation as a family. We could go down to the Oregon coast, maybe visit Portland."

I stared at her. I bet she was picturing driving down the coast singing show tunes and having some sort of family bonding moment. Our last family vacation had been a nightmare where we traveled from Walmart to Walmart while my dad worked a fake return scam. It wasn't the kind of vacation full of happy memories.

"I'm not sure I can get time off," I said. It seemed a better excuse then telling my mom I would rather be tied to the bumper and dragged behind the car than go on another family vacation. "Do you know where my baby pictures are?" I asked, steering her away from the vacation topic.

"Did you look in the shoe box?" Mom took another slice and flicked the mushrooms off.

"Yes, I looked in the box. There's a bunch of stuff in there, but no baby pictures."

"Well, I don't know where they are then." Mom tossed her slice back down and stared at me with her mouth pressed into a thin line. "So, let me guess, the fact that I don't have baby pictures is a sign that I'm a bad mother."

I stared at her with my mouth open. Parents freak out at the most random things. "Um. No. I just wanted to find some of my baby pictures. I thought maybe you knew if there were photos kept someplace other than the box."

"There were a bunch of photos that got ruined when the crawl space flooded when the sewer line broke. I threw out a couple boxes of things. Your baby pictures might have been in there."

You had to love the symbolism, the entire record of my babyhood flooded with sewage and tossed away.

"Did you talk to Thomas about staying on in the fall?" Mom reached forward and grabbed her pizza slice back. "He should be able to find you something in the hotel."

"I'm not convinced I'll be here in the fall." I couldn't believe my mom thought I was going to give up that easy. I hadn't even considered calling Thomas yet, even though I liked him. He had worked at the hotel for something like forty years. Unlike the owner and some of the other managers, he was from the island. He wasn't the kind of person who figured that because he was your manager he was some sort of god.

"Well, don't leave it for too long. They're going to let summer staff go in a few weeks, and everyone will be jockeying for a position. If you aren't careful, there won't be anything for you and you'll be stuck having to get a job over in the city."

I opened my mouth to tell her that missing out on a position at the hotel wasn't exactly a great loss, but then something occurred to me. Thomas would have been working at the hotel when Ava was taken. If there was anyone who would have dirt on what had happened behind the scenes, it would be him. Nothing happened in that hotel that he didn't know about. Nothing.

I stretched over and gave my mom a hug. She looked shocked.

"What was that for?" she asked.

"Because you're right. I do need to talk to Thomas. I'm going to do it first thing tomorrow."

chapter ten

The Keppler Hotel was built in 1922. It was huge, with over three hundred rooms, four ballrooms, two restaurants, a tearoom, a pool, a glassed-in sunporch stuffed with white wicker furniture, and a lobby that stretched over a hundred feet, with clusters of sofas and chairs in red paisley fabric. Each table had a vase with a giant floral arrangement that had to be changed every four days. Entire hothouses must have been dedicated to growing flowers for the Keppler. The front desk was carved, polished cedar, and at the end of the lobby was a fireplace the size of a minivan.

Since there weren't many places like it, several movies had been filmed at the hotel. There was a horror film, a cheesy love story, and a political thriller. Two years ago they filmed a historical movie, and most people on the island had gotten to be extras. Being in a movie is a lot less fun than you might think. I'd sat on the front porch sipping tea in a peacock green Victorian gown for hours. I'd thought my bladder was going to blow up before they finally gave me a bathroom break. I watched the movie when it came out, but I never saw myself. So much for my big Hollywood break.

I slipped in the side door off the lobby. Mr. Stanbury, the general manager, didn't like staff to be in the hotel if we weren't working. I think he was afraid he might not recognize us if we weren't in uniform and might accidentally be nice to us. The makeup sales convention must have ended, because there were lines of women checking out and clucking about wanting to be sure they made the ten a.m. ferry. Each woman appeared to be traveling with at least six suitcases the size of a small SUV. The porters in their bandleader-styled uniforms were hustling around, working up a sweat. I caught one of them and asked if he knew where to find Thomas. He pointed me toward the tearoom.

I waved to some of the waitstaff setting up for the high tea that afternoon. It didn't matter how good the scones with cream were, I couldn't imagine wanting hot tea on a day like this. Thomas sat toward the back at one of the tiny round tables with his adding machine and a stack of receipts. He squinted at a piece of paper then smiled when he saw me approach.

"Tell me what the number is there." He handed me the receipt.

I glanced down before passing it back. "A hundred forty-three dollars and sixty-four cents."

"Why people have to write so small you need a telescope to see it is a mystery to me." Thomas's fingers sped over the adding machine, tallying up the numbers.

"Maybe you should get glasses," I suggested.

"You calling me old?" Thomas raised one bushy eyebrow.

"Never." I raised a hand as if swearing a vow. "Clearly these receipts are written by miniature evil elves using tiny little ball-point pens."

Thomas laughed and waved for me to sit down. "Don't be ridiculous. Everyone knows elves use fountain pens. Now, what brings you over here on a day off? Other than making fun of me." Over a hundred people on staff, and Thomas still managed to know everyone's work schedule. If he hadn't worked at the hotel, he could have run a small country.

"I wanted to ask you about something that happened at the hotel a long time ago."

"That's me, official hotel historian." Thomas waved at one of the waiters and held up two fingers. The waiter scurried off and brought back two frosted glasses of iced tea with a mint sprig floating on top. "It's raspberry flavored. My treat. They use fresh crushed berries picked over at Harbor Farm." He took a deep drink and leaned back. "Now, what can I tell you?"

"Do you remember when Ava McKenna went missing?"

His eyebrows shot up to his hairline. "You know how to pick out a happy memory. That sure was a lousy time. I was the front desk manager back then. At first we just assumed the kid wandered off. You know how kids are at that age. If you don't have them duct taped down, they're off and running, sticking forks in light sockets, or chewing on something they shouldn't. Anyway, I had some of the waiters from the restaurant do a sweep of the hotel for her. A few months before she went missing, we had a little kid who had curled up underneath one of those heavy velvet curtains in the lobby and gone to sleep. We didn't find him until almost an hour later when he woke up. Little bugger peed his pants too while he slept, so we had to have the rugs steam cleaned."

Before he could get off track with other missing kid stories, I asked another question. "When did you realize that something was really wrong in Ava's situation?"

"After the first half hour or so I suspected we were in trouble. There wasn't a sign anywhere of where she had gone and the nanny was practically hysterical. We called the police and sent one of the managers down to the docks to wait for the parents to come back in. They were out sailing if I remember right. Not many people had cell phones back then, so there was no way to reach them out on the boat. Not that anyone was looking forward to having that conversation anyway. How do you tell someone their kid is just gone? To be honest, I didn't think someone had taken her. At that point I figured something bad had happened to her, that we were going to find her at the bottom of the pool, or having fallen off a balcony somewhere." Thomas shrugged as if he didn't know what else to add. "But when she never showed up, not even a body, I figured someone took her. This island isn't that big, and she was a small kid."

"So you think someone took her. How come there was never a demand for ransom?" I sipped the tea and fought the urge to press the frosty glass to the side of my face.

"Someone grabbed that kid, you can count on that." Thomas pointed at me with his glass for emphasis, as if I had expressed doubt. "If she had just wandered off, we would have found her. She was only three years old, for crying out loud; how far could she have gotten on her own?"

"Then what happened to her? Why hasn't there ever been any hint about where she went? If someone took her, they must have had a reason."

Thomas shrugged. "I always figured there was more to the story. Family with that much money, you would expect someone to hit them up for a big payout. Since they didn't, it could mean it was just some sicko who had a thing for kids, or it could have been someone who wanted revenge on the family."

That was a whole new angle I hadn't even thought of. "Who would want revenge on the McKenna family?"

My question amused him. "Well, who died and made you Sherlock Holmes all of a sudden?" Thomas laughed. The waiter slipped a plate with miniature lemon curd tarts onto our table and motioned I should take one. Thomas popped a whole tart into his mouth. "Or since you're a girl, are you going for an Agatha Christie sort of angle?"

"I saw something recently about it being the fifteenth anniversary of her going missing, and I realized I didn't know much about the situation. Maybe it was the idea of her and me being the same age got me interested." I wondered if Thomas had ever seen the age-enhanced photo. It was clear if he had, he hadn't seen any resemblance, but then again he wouldn't have been looking for one.

"Well, you're not the only one interested in all this past history. You should talk to that fellow from the foundation if you want details. He'd likely know more than I would. He's here at the hotel somewhere doing some of the groundwork for the big charity ball."

"What fellow?"

Thomas scrunched up his face while he pulled the detail from his mind. "His name is Chase Parker. He works with that McKenna children's charity. They're doing a big event on the island to mark the anniversary. We've got something like twenty-five media people checking into the hotel, not to mention over a hundred bigwigs from the city. They're hosting a charity fundraising dinner that night with some sort of formal announcement about a bunch of hefty donations."

I made a mental note to find Chase Parker. If he was working with the McKenna Foundation, it was possible that he would know the family, too. A little inside information never hurt. "Maybe I'll splurge for a ticket to the event," I said. "Do my part to help missing children."

"Only if you've been saving up your tip money. Tickets are something like five hundred bucks a pop." Thomas swallowed another small tart. "Course, the other person you should talk to is your mom."

I sat up straighter. "My mom?"

"Sure. She was the one who cleaned the McKennas' rooms when they were here. The police asked her a whole bunch of stuff about the family, and if she'd seen anything. The woman who worked in human resources back then made the police transcribe the whole thing for your mom's employment record. I think she was afraid the police were going to accuse your mom of doing something. She wanted to make sure the hotel didn't get dragged into the whole mess. Near as I can tell, they should just call HR 'AC,' for ass coverage."

My mind was spinning. "My mom was a suspect?"

Thomas looked at me, his face flushed with embarrassment. "Oh lord, no. I didn't mean to imply there was anything your mom did wrong." I guess he was afraid I might be offended if he smeared my only law-abiding relative. "No, your mom wasn't a suspect; they just wanted some information on the McKenna family. Course, it isn't popular to say, especially when the family is well connected like that, but in most of these cases, the family is involved. Usually it turns out that maybe the dad had a thing for little girls, or the mom drank in the afternoons and couldn't cope with the kid's crying, that kind of thing." Thomas sounded very knowledgeable about criminal motivation, as only someone who watches *Law & Order* every night could be.

"Was there ever any indication the family was involved?" If Ava's parents did have something to do with her going missing, it certainly was going to change the whole dynamic of any con I was planning.

Thomas waved away my concern. "Nah. I don't think so. The mum and dad were gutted when it happened. I can still remember the mum screaming Ava's name. I don't think you can fake emotion like that. I think there was some question about some cousin on his side who was kinda shifty. He had a whole pile of gambling debts to all the wrong people."

"But if he took Ava for money, then he would have had to make a ransom demand."

"Unless he took her to punish his family for not helping him out, or if the mob guys he owed money to took her as a lesson. He didn't have any kids of his own." Thomas leaned back and tossed up his hands in defeat. "The whole situation was weird. It was like the kid just disappeared into thin air. No ransom note, no body, no nothing. Everyone kept thinking they would find something, but everything came up empty. There were a whole bunch of theories, and even some wacky psychic who kept claiming she was getting messages from the beyond from Ava, but nothing came of any of it."

"What about the nanny? Wasn't she the one with Ava when it happened?"

Thomas rubbed his chin. "The police checked her out, but

she had a stellar employment record with the McKennas, and there didn't seem to be any motivation. She ended up losing her job when Ava went missing."

I glanced at Thomas. His mouth was scrunched up, which only happened when something was bothering him. "Anything else about her?"

"Nah. Nothing really. Can't say just because you don't like someone that they've done anything wrong."

"Why didn't you like her?" I asked.

"No reason really. Maybe I was mad she didn't like me." He smiled. "She was a looker. I invited her to a staff party that was going on while she was here. I figured she might like a night out. It's got to be lonely being a nanny in a situation like that. You're not a part of the family, you're clearly the hired help, but you spend all your time with them."

"I take it she didn't take you up on your offer?"

"She looked at me like she had just stepped in something nasty. She made it very clear that she wasn't interested." Thomas shrugged. "Don't get me wrong, it wasn't just that she turned me down for a date; it was like she wasn't interested in anything to do with any of the staff here. A few of the girls that worked the desk invited her to something and she shot them down too."

"Maybe she was just a loner."

"Could be. At any rate, the police didn't look at her too hard."

I started a mental to-do list based on what I'd learned from Thomas. Investigating the psychic would be an interesting angle.

If she'd staked her psychic reputation on getting messages from a dead Ava, she wouldn't want a live one to show up. I also needed to check up on Mr. McKenna's shifty cousin. If he owed money to loan sharks in the Seattle area, then my dad might know them. There are times when hanging around with the wrong crowd comes in handy.

I also needed to figure out how to pump my mom for information without her knowing why I wanted it. Lastly, I needed to hunt down Chase from the missing kid foundation and see if he had any other information on the family or the abduction that might help. With every heartbeat, I could feel the clock ticking down to the August first date, when my school money was due. So far, all I had was a plan to make a plan. If Brendan and I couldn't come up with an angle to the con soon, then all this information on the mysterious missing Ava wasn't going to do me any good.

Thomas snapped his fingers and I jumped. "Earth to Sadie," he said with a chuckle. I must have missed what he was saying.

"Oh, sorry, I was just thinking." I drank down the rest of the tea. "I should get going so you can finish up these receipts. Otherwise people will see you hunched over all this paperwork for the rest of the night and think you have no life."

Thomas pushed the pile of receipts on the table into a tidy stack. "Life isn't what other people think of you; it's what you get accomplished. Keeping this place running isn't too shabby of a legacy."

"The Keppler would fall down if it weren't for you," I agreed, getting up from the table.

Thomas waved me off. "Nah. It would keep standing. Now mind you, it wouldn't run nearly as well."

"Or be as fashionable," I added.

Thomas threw his napkin at me. "Go on, get out of here. Go pick on someone else."

I blew him a kiss and waved to the waitstaff as I left. Thomas might tell me to get out of here, but he had no idea how far I was willing to go to get off this island. I could only hope the information he gave me was going to help.

chapter eleven

If the McKenna Foundation was going to do a big media event, then I was willing to bet they were planning to use the Arbutus Ballroom. It was the largest of the four, they could easily get three hundred people in there, and the floor-to-ceiling windows looked out over a cliff, so the views were amazing.

I peeked into the Arbutus room. The curtains were drawn and the lights were off. I could see there were stacks of chairs in the corner waiting to be set up, a few tables with tablecloths sprinkled around, and a pile of audio equipment at the front.

There was a sound behind me and I heard people coming up the stairs. "If you head this way, Mr. Parker, you can see the room."

Shit! It was Mr. Stanbury, the general manager. If he saw me here, he was going to yell at me for being on the property.

Not to mention, I didn't want to meet Mr. Parker wearing a T-shirt and flip-flops. That probably wouldn't make him want to spill his guts to me. I yanked up the tablecloth and dove under the closest table just before they came around the corner.

"We'll set up the tables for the guests over here," Stanbury said. I heard the screech of the curtains being pulled back. "Depending on the weather, we can open up all of these French doors and people can mingle on the patio as well. We typically suggest setting up at least two buffet and bar stations with a crowd this size."

"The McKennas would prefer to use waitstaff versus having a buffet. They don't want guests waiting in a line."

"Not a problem. We'll arrange staff to circulate with hors d'oeuvres and to bring cocktails." Stanbury snapped his fingers, and I suspected his secretary was trailing after him taking notes. Being Stanbury's secretary would be its own special level of hell. I would rather clean toilets with my tongue than have to spend my days saying, "Yes, sir, right away, sir," to feed his ego.

"Is it possible to set up a screen? I'd like to have a slide show running during part of the event, some photos of Ava, but also of the children the foundation has been able to reunite with their families."

"Brilliant idea," Stanbury said. The only thing that he liked more than people kissing his ass was a chance for him to kiss the asses of the rich and powerful. "I'd be happy to assist you with organizing the media if you like." Stanbury gave a chuckle. "In my position, I've had a lot of experience."

"I couldn't ask you to be a media spokesman on top of your already massive duties," Mr. Parker said with a flat voice. I would have high-fived him for giving the smack down to Mr. Stanbury except for the fact that I was hiding under a table. "The McKennas have provided me with clear directives on how they would like the media handled. As you might imagine, they would like to keep the focus on the positive action of the foundation, not on a sensationalist review of the loss of their daughter."

"Of course not," Mr. Stanbury said. "Would you like to take another look at the menu?"

"No. I was happy with the menu that was finalized last week. I would like to review options for when the guests arrive. I'd like to figure out how we can have people pre–checked in, especially our VIP guests."

"We can do that. We also typically arrange to have fresh flowers in those rooms or perhaps a fruit basket with champagne."

I shifted my cramped legs as silently as possible.

"We'll need the list of guests and what you would like in each gift basket at least a day before everyone arrives."

"I'll have the list for you tomorrow."

"Excellent. I'll arrange to have examples of the various table linen options brought to your room so that you can choose what you would like used for the event."

There were some shuffling sounds and then silence. I made myself count to two hundred to give them time to get down the hall, then I crawled out from under the table and stood.

"Well, I can't say I expected that," a voice said behind me.

I spun around. The voice belonged to Chase Parker. This really wasn't the way I'd wanted to meet him. But as soon as I saw him, the excuses I was about to make dried up on my tongue. "*You're* Chase Parker?" He was nothing like what I'd expected. I'd assumed he would be a slick businessman in his forties or fifties. One of those guys who wears his thinning hair slicked back and a suit that cost more than most people spend on food in a year. But Chase was young. I guessed he wasn't much older than me. He was wearing tailored chinos and a loose linen shirt. Not that I was paying much attention to his clothes. I was too distracted by the fact that he was beautiful. Not attractive—Chase was stunning, model-perfect, drop-your-panties kind of good-looking. He looked like an angel from one of the Italian paintings we'd studied in art appreciation. He had honey blond hair, wide blue eyes with eyelashes that went on forever, and his mouth would make Angelina Jolie envious. I wanted to touch his lips, they were so perfect.

"You have me at a bit of a disadvantage. You seem to know me, but I don't know you," he said.

"Me?"

Chase laughed. Even his teeth were perfect, blindingly white and ruler straight. Either he had great genes or his parents had spent a fortune on orthodontic care. "Asking who you were wasn't supposed to be a trick question."

"Sadie." I mentally kicked myself. So much for giving him a fake name. I wasn't off to a great start with my plan to schmooze him into telling me everything I needed to know about the McKenna family. I held my breath. He was looking directly at my face, but there wasn't a hint of recognition. Brendan was right: The fact that I'd dyed my hair dark was enough to change my appearance from the MISSING poster, that and the fact that no one really expected to spot Ava. They all must have assumed she'd died. Well, everyone except her parents.

"So, Sadie, be honest. Are you a runaway who secretly lives in the hotel, sleeping under tables and surviving only on stolen restaurant food?" he asked with a smile.

"No." I thought quickly and decided to play along. "Actually, underneath the table there's a portal to an alternate universe. I don't want to brag or anything, but I'm sort of a messiah there, charged with finding the magical ring and saving all of mankind," I said.

He raised an eyebrow. "That's a heavy load for someone who is . . . seventeen?"

"I'm eighteen and I was always an overachiever. Saving humanity is only a hobby," I went on. "You should see the stuff I'm working on full-time."

"I'd like that." He smiled and my stomach fluttered in appreciation. Then I remembered that I was supposed to be pumping him for information. My mind spun around, looking for the right angle.

"It's funny you say that. I'm with a local island group dedicated to involving youth in social service projects. I'm really impressed with the work the McKenna Foundation is doing and wondered if there might be a way to assist you with your plans for the event here."

"What a great idea, getting students involved. I believe if you get involved early in life with volunteering, you stay with it. I've never heard of organized student volunteer groups, but more people should do it."

He'd never heard of this group because I'd just made it up a couple of seconds ago. "We're firm believers that a commitment to public service starts young." I tried to project a positive "be all you can be" type image. "I wonder if I could talk with you about how we might be able to help." I left off the fact that any information he could give me would be helping me far more than my imaginary service group would be helping him.

"Sure. How about I buy you a cup of coffee downstairs?"

"Uh . . ." I couldn't take the chance of meeting with him inside the hotel. All the staff knew me. If they overheard me talking about being some sort of community leader, they were going to start laughing. Plus, if Mr. Stanbury saw me, he would give me a lecture and ask me to leave. "I've actually already had so much coffee. Why don't we take a walk outside? They've got a boardwalk that goes along the beach."

"Sounds good." He gestured for me to lead the way. We went down the side staircase, and when we opened the door to the outside, I took a deep breath of relief, right up until he spoke again. "So you have to tell me the real reason you were under the table."

chapter twelve

Not that I am advocating lying, but if you want to do it well, there are a few things to keep in mind:

- Keep it simple. The more you say, the more opportunities there are for you to contradict yourself.
- Keep it as close to the truth as possible; it will make it easier to remember.
- The secret to being believed when lying is that you have to believe in the lie just a little bit yourself. Not that you don't know you're lying, but perhaps the lie you're telling is something that you wish were true.

Now I simply needed to come up with a reason for hiding under a table that met these criteria, and didn't make me sound like a complete nut.

"The truth is, the hotel manager and I don't get along very well," I said, going for the truth, if not the full truth. "My family has some . . . connections to the hotel, and there have been some incidents that make things uncomfortable." I waved my hand dismissively. "It isn't that my family doesn't think Mr. Stanbury's a good manager, but he tends to have quite the ego. He sometimes forgets that he works at the hotel; he doesn't own it. I knew if he heard me asking you about the event, he would try to discourage our group from getting involved. If the event goes well, he wants all the glory to go to the hotel and him."

Chase nodded. "I know the type. The kind who has to take credit for everything, including things they had nothing to do with."

"Exactly." I felt the tight band around my chest loosen. He believed me.

"He probably feels he has something to prove. He's probably one of those guys who can't stand people who have money, like our families didn't work hard to get where they are."

I nodded, as if I had any idea what it was like to have so much money that other people judged me for it. Pesky poor people. "So now that you know about me, you have to tell me how you got involved with the McKenna Foundation. You're younger than I was expecting. When I heard someone was coming over to organize the event, I pictured the typical business manager type."

"I was hoping to impress you with my overachiever status. I'm only twenty, you know. Or were you hoping for an older man? I'm crushed." He pressed his hand to chest as if I had wounded him.

I gave him a soft punch in the shoulder. He fended me off and then linked my arm through his elbow. It seemed gallant and old-fashioned, but I couldn't tell if it was meant to be polite or flirting.

"My family knows the McKennas," Chase admitted. "My mom and Mrs. McKenna were roommates back at Vassar. I've been helping out with the foundation since I was a kid. My major in college is communications, so they arranged for me to have this job for the summer. I'm organizing this event and a 10K run they sponsor at the end of August, plus helping the communications director with any press releases, that kind of thing." He looked over at me. "Admit it, you're blown away by the glory of my unpaid internship."

It sounded more glamorous than passing out salad dressing to hotel guests, but I was willing to bet Chase Parker didn't have a lot of manual labor job experience. "It's great they gave you the job." It was great for me at least. Spending time with Chase was way better than sucking up to some old guy with hair growing out of his ears.

"The McKennas are amazing. What happened to them, with their daughter, Ava, was terrible. I was really young when it happened, but I can still remember bits and pieces of it. They turned their personal tragedy into a chance to help others. So many people don't make it through that kind of thing. Did you know something like seventy percent of couples who lose a child end up divorced? And the problem is huge. The National Center for

Missing and Exploited Children estimates more than seven hundred thousand juveniles were reported missing last year."

"No, I didn't know that, Mr. Communications Director."

Chase laughed. "Sorry. Hazard of the job. I start talking like a public service announcement."

"What made them want to do this big event now? Ava's been missing for years."

"I think for them, time is measured in what could have been, milestones that aren't actually being reached, but they still think about it anyway. Ava would have been eighteen this year. She would have graduated from high school. She'd be heading off to college in the fall. They can't help but imagine what school she would have picked, if she would have been more like her mom, or if she would have been a sports nut like her dad. They wanted to do something to mark the occasion, maybe let the universe know they haven't forgotten."

I guessed since she was only three when she disappeared, it's all about imagining what she would have been like. They can't really miss who she was, since she never really got a chance to be anyone.

We walked without saying anything and instead watched the kids who were playing on the beach, sitting on bright candy-colored towels, scooping sand into pails and then dumping it out, or running up to the water and screeching when the waves licked at their feet, all under the watchful eyes of their moms, siblings, or babysitters.

"It must be hard for them, the not knowing," I said. "Was there ever any clue about what really happened?"

"The FBI is fairly sure she was abducted. There were witnesses who saw a man walking away from the hotel with a girl that might have been Ava."

My ears pricked up. This hadn't been in the newspaper reports. "I never heard that."

Chase shrugged. "No one ever identified the guy. Three witnesses saw him, but he was with two small children, not just one, so it's quite possible it was some dad with his kids. No one was even sure it was really Ava to start with, and then you factor in that eyewitnesses are really unreliable and you don't have much to go on. A few years ago they thought they might have found her stuffed rabbit."

"Rabbit?"

"It was a detail the police didn't release in case they ever needed something that could verify a real lead versus some crackpot. You wouldn't believe the number of people who call in with tips, or claiming to be the person who took a child, or know who did."

"People confessed to a crime they didn't do?" I motioned for us to sit on one of the painted benches that lined the sandy beach. There was a small tree next to it so there was even a hint of shade.

Chase sat down and rolled up his pants, sticking his legs into the sun. "Yeah. I don't get it either. I guess I'd have to major in psychology to sort that out. A lot of people accuse their exes, but that I can at least understand. Why anyone would want to say they did something just to get attention seems bizarre to me."

"So what was the deal with the rabbit?" I asked. This was exactly the kind of small detail that might make a huge difference to any con.

"Ava had this stuffed rabbit. She called it—"

"Bun Bun," I said.

"How did you know that?"

I started. How had I known that? It had come to me out of nowhere. "I had a stuffed bunny when I was a kid, and that's what I called it," I admitted. I felt uneasy. There was something eerie about the fact that Ava and I each had our own stuffed bunny with the same name.

"Must be the stuffed bunny equivalent of a name like Bob Smith. Anyway, Ava dragged that rabbit everywhere. If she didn't have it, she would scream. Apparently her parents bought a duplicate bunny in case the original Bun Bun was lost."

"Sort of a bunny body double."

"Exactly. Except Ava could tell he was an imposter bunny. It was the original Bun Bun or nothing. She would carry him around by one ear, and when she was stressed she would rub the ear against her face." Chase rolled his eyes.

"Hey, I used to do that with my stuffed rabbit too. Don't mock it if you haven't tried it. It can be very soothing." I wagged my finger in his face.

Chase held up his hands in surrender. "What a girl does with her bunny is her business. Anyway, the stuffed bunny went missing just a few hours before Ava did. The nanny reported it was missing to the front desk, hoping someone had turned it in. You can imagine what kind of crisis this was. Ava was apparently freaking out. She was a girl who had serious bunny dependence issues."

"So she must have dropped it somewhere?"

"That's the weird thing. The bunny went missing in the morning, but they hadn't been anywhere that day yet. No one knows how the bunny went missing. One of the theories was that the kidnapper somehow took the rabbit and used that to lure her away."

I felt a ripple of disgust roll over my skin. Something about the idea of someone using a kid's stuffed toy to make her feel safe when they were planning to hurt her was just nasty.

"A year or two ago someone mailed the foundation a stuffed bunny. No note or anything. So the McKennas freaked out and wondered if it was supposed to be some sort of message or something. Maybe at long last the kidnapper was going to tell them where to find Ava, or at least her body. The police tried to hunt down who sent the bunny, but nothing. The package was dropped off at a post office in downtown Portland, Oregon, and paid for in cash. No one remembers anything about who dropped it off. There was nothing about the paper or box that had any real leads. The manufacturer hadn't made that model of stuffed rabbit for years, so whoever sent it hadn't bought it recently. Dead end. The McKennas waited to see if there would be a note or anything else later, but nothing. Just a stuffed bunny that looked like the one that used to belong to their daughter."

"Is there some way to test the bunny and figure out if it was hers? DNA or something?" I watched *CSI*; it seemed like they could test anything these days. On TV they were always finding clues from the most bizarre things. I could picture all sorts of white-lab-coated professionals looking over the bunny with microscopic precision.

"They knew it wasn't Ava's—it was too pristine—but it was the same style. The tricky thing is, people send toys to the foundation all the time. We work with kids, so there's nothing weird about that." Chase shrugged. "The whole thing could be nothing more than a coincidence. Someone bought the rabbit a long time ago, then they cleaned out a closet and donated it."

"I guess." Chase was right. People tend to find meanings in all sorts of things that are just random. It's one of the reasons so many cons work.

"Enough depressing talk. The day is too nice. Tell me more about you." Chase tapped my knee. It was a casual touch, but a jolt of electricity shot up my leg.

I looked up into his face to see if he could tell the effect he was having on me. He stared into my eyes as if he couldn't wait for whatever I might be about to say. I felt as if my skin had developed some kind of superpower where it could measure the exact distance between the two of us. I was supposed to be thinking about the con I needed to pull, and instead I was thinking, *What would he do if I just leaned over and kissed him?*

"Hey! Fancy seeing you here."

I nearly fell off the bench in shock. Brendan was standing in front of us. I'd been so focused on Chase, I hadn't seen or heard him coming.

I stood up before Brendan could say anything more, anything that might hint that I wasn't the kind of person who had hotel-owning parents and spent her spare time on charity work. "Brendan, this is Chase Parker. He's organizing the McKenna Foundation event."

Brendan's eyes sparked as he realized who was in front of him. "Welcome to Bowton Island."

"We've been talking about how the youth service group could help." I raised my eyebrows at Brendan, but I didn't have to worry. We'd followed each other's leads with far more complicated cons in the past. "Chase, this is Brendan. He's my cousin."

"You'd be lucky to get her help," Brendan said, careful not to use my real name in case I had given Chase a different one. "She's a whiz at these kinds of things."

"Well, I probably should head back now, but how about I take you out for dinner to discuss it?" Chase asked, and my heart sped up a bit. A date.

"Your boyfriend isn't going to like that idea," Brendan said, smiling at me. "You know how jealous he gets."

If I could have shot poison darts from my eyes, Brendan

would have dropped to the ground and foamed at the mouth before he died a slow, painful death. "Very funny, Cuz." I turned to Chase. "He's joking. He's my practical joke cousin. I don't have a boyfriend. I'd love to meet up for dinner."

"Great. I'm guessing you don't want to eat at the hotel," Chase said. "I saw an Italian place in town. Would that work? I could pick you up around six thirty?"

"Tortuffo's. They've got great risotto." I snapped my fingers like something had just occurred to me. "You know what, I have to run some errands later today. It might be better if I met you there." No way I was going to let Chase pick me up at my trailer.

"Hey, do you smoke?" Brendan asked Chase.

Chase looked slightly confused. "No. Sorry."

"Oh, me neither. I just picked up a pack of cigarettes because this guy on the ferry was telling me it was possible to tie a cigarette in a knot without it tearing or falling apart." Brendan pulled out a pack of Marlboros and tossed them in the air, catching them. "I was going to try to figure out if it could be done."

"There's no way. They would tear for sure," Chase said.

I stepped forward and caught the cigarette pack on Brendan's next toss. I'd seen Brendan do the cigarette con at least a dozen times. There was no way I was going to let him cheat Chase out of five or ten bucks. "Of course there's no way it could be done. You'd better not let your dad see you with cigarettes. You know how he feels about that." I stared him down.

Brendan smiled, but I could see the annoyance in his eyes.

"Yeah, you're probably right. Most likely the guy was trying to con me out of some money." He slid the cigarettes back into his pocket. "So, I came looking for you because we're supposed to go do that stuff for Aunt Millicent, Cuz." He drew out the last word.

"I'm sure we could do it later," I said.

"Oh you know how Auntie can be." Brendan shook his head and turned to Chase. "Our aunt Millicent is a hundred and one years old. She's actually our great-aunt. She's got this china doll collection that's amazing. A whole room full of shelves stacked from floor to ceiling with dolls."

"You're right, she will worry," I said, cutting him off before he could come up with more elaborate stories. I squeezed Chase's arm. "I'll meet up with you later."

"No problem. I should get back to work anyway. I've got to pick out the right table linens."

"You wouldn't want wrong linens," Brendan said in a fake chummy voice. "Imagine the horror." I wanted to ninja kick him in the knees.

"See you later." Chase gave me a smile that melted my desire to whack Brendan with a bat. He shook Brendan's hand. "Nice to meet you."

Brendan and I watched Chase walk back toward the hotel.

"Aunt Millicent?" I hissed when Chase was far enough away.

"Cousins?" Brendan countered with a raised eyebrow.

chapter thirteen

Brendan followed me home. He wanted to look through the information I'd already gathered on the McKenna family. I never used to care if he was in my room with me, but ever since we'd been together it felt weird. Now I didn't want to sit with him on my bed, but there wasn't any other space in my room, so I dragged everything outside onto the broken-down picnic table in our yard.

Brendan sat down carefully. "The only thing this table is good for anymore is making splinters. You touch it and it imbeds wood into your hand." Brendan lightly touched the surface of the scarred table. "It's a terrorist table. The United States could drop this into a war zone as some kind of weapon."

I dumped the pile of information and pictures I'd printed off the Internet onto the tabletop. "If it's giving you splinters, then don't touch it."

"Somebody's cranky." Brendan flipped through the stack of papers.

I decided to ignore him. I managed to stay quiet all of a few minutes. "I'm not cranky. I just didn't need you trying to con the guy I need information from with one of your two-bit cigarette bets."

Brendan looked up from what he was reading and raised an eyebrow. "Uh-huh." He looked back down.

I sat on the edge of the seat and bounced my foot up and down in annoyance while he read. Brendan was the master of driving me nuts. He could get a PhD in irritating behavior without having to study.

I reached for a newspaper article and a splinter sliced into the pad of my fingertip, burying itself into my flesh. I snatched my hand back. I stuck my finger in my mouth and sucked on it, trying to pull the sliver of wood out. I glanced across the table and saw Brendan smirking.

"So are you happy now?" I asked him. "You're right. The table has some kind of splinter jihad going."

Brendan shrugged and looked back through the stacks of paper. I spun the ring on my finger in irritation.

"Don't think I don't know that you were pulling the con on Chase because you don't like him," I said.

Brendan rolled his eyes. "Rich people call their kids weird stuff. Who the hell names their kid Chase? It's like that movie star who named her kid Apple."

"You don't like him because of his name?" I crossed my arms. "Well, that makes sense. Very mature."

"The issue isn't what I think of him; it's what *you* think of him. You like him. You should have seen yourself, flipping your hair around, leaning in whenever he said anything." Brendan pressed one hand to his heart and the other to his forehead. "Oh, Chase," he said, in a fake girly voice. "You're so smart and clever! Why, I would love to have dinner with you. I can't imagine what else I would rather do."

If not for the fact that a thousand splinters would have sliced me to death, I would have reached across the table and smacked Brendan. "Like you've never flirted to get what you wanted? Besides, I've never been anything but honest with you. I don't know why you're surprised I would go out with someone else. If you want to pretend that we're destined to be more than friends, that's fine, but you shouldn't be upset that I don't share that delusion."

Brendan barked out a laugh. "I'm delusional? What about your delusion? You think this guy likes you? You think he would have anything to do with you if he knew you came from here?" Brendan's arm swept around. "The person he asked out for dinner doesn't exist. You made her up, some rich girl who spends her time doing charity when she isn't planning to head off to the Ivy League. He's not interested in you, he's interested in your con."

"Oh, please, and what about all the stories you tell to get summer girls into bed? Didn't you convince some stupid slut last year that you were in the witness protection program? That you were living under a death sentence?"

Brendan smiled as if this was a fond memory. "I told her I'd given evidence to put a mobster away in prison for life. I knew it was dangerous, but I had to do the right thing; innocent people deserve justice. She wanted to make sure I had a happy memory, since it was likely they would catch up to me someday and take me out in a hail of gunfire."

"Hail of gunfire? Nice touch. I suppose next you'll pretend you have some sort of terminal illness and want to know the love of a good woman before you breathe your last. Maybe you could ask the Make-A-Wish Foundation to help you get some cheap tail."

Brendan held up a hand to cut me off. "Whoa up. She wasn't cheap. I'll give you that she wasn't that smart, but I took her out to dinner at least two or three times. Nothing cheap about that girl."

"You're disgusting," I said.

"Maybe, but I'm honest. I always knew the whole thing was fake. The problem is that you seem to be forgetting it. You want to tell Mr. Fancy Pants some story to get what you want, fine by me. Hell, I'll help you make the story better. But don't lie to yourself." Brendan's eyes locked with mine. "When you start lying to yourself, it's just sad."

I wanted to get up from the table and run around screaming. Maybe pick up one of Ms. Flick's plastic garden gnomes and hurl it at Brendan. I enjoyed the image of bashing him in the head with one of the gnomes' pointy red hats. He went back to ignoring me, reading through the printouts. Brendan's hand suddenly slapped down on a stack of paper and he let out a whoop.

"What?" I leaned forward.

Brendan's smile spread across his face. He looked like a kid who'd wandered downstairs and caught Santa Claus unloading a heap of giant presents under his tree. He waved a newspaper article at me. "Here's the angle on your con."

I grabbed the article out of his hand and skimmed through it. It was an interview with the McKennas' nanny about what had happened. Nothing stuck out to me. I couldn't figure out what had caught his attention.

"Don't you see it?" Brendan asked.

I read the article again, and then it leaped off the page at me. The nanny stated that she was in the McKennas' suite, but she left because the maid had wanted to clean the room. She took a napping Ava in the stroller outside, and while she was looking out at the water, Ava either climbed out of the stroller or was taken. Brendan passed me another sheet of paper, where I had written down a timeline of events. Ava went missing between ten thirty a.m. and eleven a.m. I felt a smile slide across my face.

"No way a maid came to clean the room at that time," I said. Cleaning over three hundred hotel rooms in a day requires a system. Each night, the hotel front desk prints out a list of what rooms are due to check out the coming day. Those would be the first cleaned so that when new guests checked in they could go immediately to their rooms. Once those rooms were done, the hotel was cleaned floor by floor, starting with the second floor. The McKennas were in a suite on the top floor and weren't due to check out. No way anyone would have shown up to clean their room at 10:30 unless someone had called down and requested the room be done right away. "The nanny lied," I said.

"The nanny lied," Brendan repeated with a smile. "It wasn't an accident."

"Do you think she did something to Ava?" I pictured Nancy Goodall as she appeared on TV with her perfectly shellacked hair and bland politician-styled suits. She annoyed me, and Thomas hadn't liked her, but I hadn't thought of her as someone who would do something to a kid.

"Doubt it. My guess is that she went out to sneak a smoke or to meet a boyfriend. Something she shouldn't have been doing. She lied to cover herself, and nobody caught it. The important thing is, this woman makes millions now talking about how to protect your kids. You think anyone is going to want to buy books and safety crap from her if it comes out that she lied to cover her own ass?"

"No way." My skin tingled with excitement.

"That's a lot on the line for her. Can't see her giving up her regular gigs on the *Today* show easily. She's parlayed this whole thing into a nice career. One that's paid for some nice designer duds, a vacation property in Maui, and an expensive lifestyle. That's an awfully nice career to risk losing, especially over a kid who's been gone for years."

"I need to know more about the nanny," I said.

Brendan stood up from the table. "Now you have something to talk about with Mr. Fancy Pants over dinner."

chapter fourteen

Figuring out what to wear on my date felt more complicated than deciding what to write for my Berkeley essay. I wanted to look nice, but not like I was trying too hard. I wanted to look sexy, but not like I should be working on a street corner. The outfit needed to be classy, but not something that looked like I was trying to impress someone. People who have money can sniff out cheap clothing at a mile. If the fabric drapes incorrectly, if it pills up, or if the seams don't line up, it screams low-end mass retail. I had a few really nice things that I'd bought at a thrift store in a wealthy section of Seattle. After pulling things on and off in various combinations for a half hour, I decided on a navy blue sundress with spaghetti straps and bright red poppies along the hemline. It was a bit too dressy for the restaurant, but it was my best option.

The screen door slammed shut, and I could hear my mom kick off her shoes in the living room. Perfect. She might let me take her car so that I wouldn't have to show up for my date on my scooter. Helmet hair is not an elegant look.

"Don't you look nice," Mom said as I walked out. I did a model spin for her and posed like I was at the end of the catwalk. "Brendan certainly is a lucky young man."

I felt myself slump. My mom had wanted me to date Brendan for my entire life. "I'm not going out with Brendan. My date is a guy I met at the hotel, one of the guests. Brendan and I are just friends," I said slowly and clearly so there could be no confusion.

"Oh." She rummaged in her purse, pretending to look for something, so we could avoid discussing that awkward topic any further.

"When I was at the hotel today, I saw they were gearing up for a big charity event," I said.

Mom shrugged. "It's summer; seems like they've got something going every free moment. They had three weddings last Saturday alone."

"It's a fund-raiser. It's the anniversary of the girl who went missing fifteen years ago, Ava McKenna." I paused to see if she would jump in and mention how she'd been connected to the case.

Mom made a noncommittal sound and flopped down on the sofa. She pulled out a book with a pirate with his shirt torn off on the cover. It was unclear to me why people in romance novels are always wearing clothes that are half shredded. "You're welcome to take my car tonight if you want. I don't plan to move from this spot."

"Thanks." I shifted in place waiting for her to say something about Ava, but instead she clicked over to a rerun of *Who Wants to Be a Millionaire*. She snorted when the contestant missed an easy question. I watched her for a second and then tried to drag her back to the topic at hand. "You must have worked at the hotel when Ava went missing. I bet it was pretty exciting."

Mom didn't even turn away from the television. "I don't really remember. I guess so."

My eyebrows drew together. "You don't remember her going missing? It was the biggest thing to ever happen on this island. They had the FBI here." I waited for her to volunteer the other obvious reason she should remember: She'd been questioned by the police.

Mom shrugged. "How does someone even go on this show if they don't know something simple like that? I swear they must give a reverse intelligence test to screen contestants. If you have the sense to get yourself out of a paper bag, they pick someone else." My mom dreamed of being on a game show. Not that she ever applied, or did anything about it, other than talk about how she would win the big prizes.

"The police must have been all over everyone at the hotel, wanting to find someone who had seen something," I said, giving her another opportunity.

"I think I worked in the laundry back when that happened. I don't remember much about it." She turned the volume up a notch.

I stared at the back of her head. My mom was lying. The police had questioned her in particular. No way she had forgotten something like that.

Mom turned to face me. "I thought you had a hot date. Why are you so interested in all this ancient history all of a sudden?"

"I'm not interested," I said with a shrug. I scooped the car keys off the table by the front door. Two could play this game. I could lie just as well as she did.

chapter fifteen

Tortuffo's was one of four restaurants on the island outside the hotel. We also had a Dairy Queen, a coffee shop that made sandwiches, and the Beach Shack, which specialized in burgers and hot dogs that always had a bit of sandy grit in them. Tortuffo's was small. It only had room for about fifteen tables, and even then the waitresses had to turn to the side to snake through with their trays. You could get a pizza there, but it wasn't a pizza joint. They specialized in homemade pasta and gnocchi, along with chicken and steak. The owner greeted every guest who came in and stopped by two or three times during your dinner to ask in his thick Italian accent if your meal was good. He was actually Irish, but he did a great fake accent that fooled everyone who didn't know him.

I parked my mom's car outside the restaurant. She drove a

1974 robin's-egg blue Karmann Ghia. My dad had bought it for my mom from a junkyard before I was born, and fixed it up. Brendan's dad was a mechanic at the Keppler. He kept their cars and various landscaping machines running. As a favor to my dad, he kept the car in mint condition. At least I didn't have to be embarrassed to be seen with it. It wasn't a Lexus or BMW, but it had its own quirky style.

Chase was already inside. When I approached the table, he stood like a gentleman out of the eighteen hundreds. He was wearing jeans with a dark shirt. *Shit.* I was overdressed.

"You look great," Chase said, reaching to pull my chair out for me.

"Thanks." My nose was already twitching from the smell of garlic, roasted tomatoes, and fresh baked bread. Maybe in addition to being overdressed, I could order way more food than any one person needed and stuff it all into my face, chewing with my mouth open. That's me, born classy.

I picked at the hem on my cloth napkin, trying to think of something to say.

"How did things go with your aunt?" Chase said, looking over the options on the leather menu before giving his choice to the waiter.

My mind went blank. I couldn't remember what Brendan had called her. This was the problem with lying to someone: keeping it straight. "Um. She's good." I stared down at the menu as if it were a tricky calculus problem to be solved.

"Hey. They have fritoles for dessert. Have you had those?"

Not only had I not ever had one, I wasn't even sure what it was. But for all I knew, rich girls ate them all the time. I made a noncommittal noise.

"I spent the winter in Venice a couple years ago, and during Carnevale I must have eaten a thousand of those. I'll bet I gained twenty pounds in fried dough, raisins, and pine nuts. I haven't had one since then. Have you ever been to Venice in the off-season?"

I loved how he assumed I'd been to Venice at all. "No, I haven't."

"It's amazing. I love the city at any time. How can you not love a place where they once called their currency a sequin?" He laughed. "The city is totally different in the winter. It's cold and damp. The place isn't packed with tourists, and the streets fill with fog and make it feel like the city's been cut off from the rest of the world. It seems possible you could turn a corner and find yourself several hundred years in the past."

"It sounds perfect." I made a mental note to add Venice to my list of places I wanted to go someday. "Did you go with family or friends from school?"

Chase flushed. "It's stupid. I went by myself over winter break because I had this idea that I was going to write a book. I think I thought I was a modern-day Byron or something. I was going to write the great new American novel. I rented an apartment overlooking the Grand Canal in Salute-Punta Dogana. I brought my laptop, arranged for this local woman to bring me meals, and sat down ready to bleed onto the page."

I absolutely loved that he'd done this. It was the most romantic thing I could imagine. I didn't know anyone who had just up and rented an apartment in Europe to do anything, let alone write a book. "What happened?" I asked, leaning forward.

Chase laughed. "Turns out I had nothing to say. I started wandering the streets, drinking cups and cups of espresso in these small cafés, anything to avoid just sitting there at the desk. At first I told myself that I was soaking up the atmosphere, 'letting my muse find her way' kind of thing. Eventually I realized I wasn't fooling anyone; I wasn't a novelist."

I felt the absurd urge to defend him. "You might be. You can't expect that you would just sit down and write a novel. It's the kind of thing that takes practice. You wouldn't expect to sit down at a piano and start playing Mozart. Why would writing be any different?"

"I think I liked the idea of being an author more than I wanted to write. My problem is, I've never been really good at anything."

I opened my mouth to protest, but he raised a hand to stop me.

"Don't get me wrong, I'm not fishing for a compliment. I'm good at a lot of things. Good student, decent at lacrosse, I make a pretty good omelet, but there's nothing that I'm *really* good at. You know what I mean? Like, really good."

"Like, the reason you exist," I said.

"Exactly! I wanted to have something that was my passion. Some big grand point to my life. It seemed like everyone I knew had something. They wanted to be rock stars, or get into medical school, or this one girl I dated in high school desperately wanted to be the next Martha Stewart. She had binders full of all these recipes and craft ideas. She would videotape herself pretending to do show segments on things like quilting teapot cozies out of old baby clothing and put them up on the Internet."

"Wow. She sounds intense."

"Tell me about it. She made great cookies though," he said with a smile. "She drove me nuts, but I was fascinated by the fact that she knew what she wanted, that she was so sure."

"And now, do you know what you want to do?" I reached for one of the bread sticks at the same time he did and our hands bumped. I jumped as if an electrical charge had run through my hand.

Chase leaned back with a sigh. "No. Not really. I know I want to do something that matters. I don't want to look back and think: 'Yep, I sure owned some nice cars.' It doesn't have to be world changing, like saving all the hungry kids in Africa, but I want it to be something. In the meantime, I've decided to let up on myself and stop trying to figure out what to do with my life and instead focus on what I'm doing right now."

"Seems like a plan. The work you're doing with the foundation is important."

"That's me, charming money out of the wealthy one dollar at a time."

The waiter put our plates down. Chase had gone for pasta with various kinds of seafood. It looked exotic, but I didn't think I could bring myself to eat anything that had a tentacle. I'd ordered lasagna. I hoped that didn't make me look boring. People who rent apartments in Europe eat tentacles, and lasagna eaters consider going to Target to be a big adventure.

"Maybe being charming is the thing you're really good at, and if charming raises money and awareness for an important cause, then it's pretty important."

Chase's eyes met mine across the table. It was likely due to the candles everywhere, but his eyes actually seemed to twinkle. He nudged my foot with his. "Are you saying you think I'm charming?"

I blushed. "Now you *are* fishing for compliments." Our feet were still touching under the table. I didn't want the connection to end. If he pulled away, there was the risk I would lunge forward so I could still touch him.

"So, tell me about you. Do you know your passion? Your reason for being?" Chase swirled his fork through the pasta, winding it up. He smiled at me, and I tried to determine if he said the word "passion" with an extra emphasis or if it was my rabid imagination.

"I'm not always sure what I want. Sometimes it seems more clear what I don't want," I admitted.

"But don't you want to be going *to* something instead of running away from something?"

I put my fork down. "I'm not running away," I said sternly, to convince either him or myself. "I don't know everything I want, but I do know I want to be an architect."

"I should introduce you to Mr. McKenna," Chase offered.

My pulse jumped. "When are he and his wife coming over?"

"Just before the event. Nothing against your hometown, but as you might imagine, this isn't their favorite place. They aren't even staying the night. They chartered a boat that will take them back to Seattle after the fund-raiser."

"Who else is coming to the party?"

Chase listed off the A-list of the Seattle social scene. There were even a few celebrities coming in from California. He noticed my expression. "Celebrities attract media attention. We should bring in a million or so in donations at the event, but we'll get significantly more online from people who read or see something in the news about it. It's the follow-up donations that make the difference. We make way more in ten- and twenty-dollar donations. It all adds up."

"What about the nanny, Nancy Goodall?"

Chase grimaced. "Yeah. She wasn't invited."

"Do the McKennas blame her for what happened?"

"No. I think they blame themselves more. They felt bad for her. Nancy was distraught when Ava disappeared. She was in her twenties at the time. The McKennas let her go—they didn't need to employ a nanny when they didn't have a kid anymore. Then, of course, she couldn't find another job."

"I guess no one wants a nanny who lost her last charge. It's not very Mary Poppins–ish."

"Exactly. She started doing interviews with all those tabloid shows, because they would pay. That pissed off the McKennas, but what really set them on edge was when she started selling all that crap."

"The safety stuff?" I asked.

"The McKennas obviously support people doing whatever they can to keep their kids safe, but the idea of her making all this money based off the memory of their daughter doesn't make them too happy. The whole 'I lived through this nightmare, but you don't have to' thing sets their teeth on edge."

"Have they asked her to stop?"

"I don't know all the history, but I know they had lawyers involved at one point. There really wasn't much they could do as long as she didn't use their daughter's name in her promotional material, but she always found a way to phrase it where everyone knew who she was talking about." Chase shrugged. "Goodall makes it sound like she's still connected to the family, but they don't want a thing to do with her, and I can't blame them. Using someone else's pain to make money is pretty low."

This was good information. Chase motioned to the waiter, indicating he wanted another bottle of San Pellegrino for our table. I wondered what he would think if he knew what I was after. The con I was planning was just a different way of trying to make money off someone's pain. I watched Chase. He was the kind of person who believed in doing the right thing. Brendan would point out that having all the money in the world makes it easier to worry about what is right or wrong. I couldn't afford to feel guilty.

"Do you want some more bread sticks?" Chase asked, breaking my chain of thought.

"Not if we're going to try those Venetian fritters," I said. "And after the sell job you did, I feel like I pretty much have to try them if I can fit them in."

"Well, if you can't fit enough of them in tonight, we'll just have to come back."

My heart sped up at his casual mention of another date. He wanted to see me again. What made me nervous was that I wanted to see him again too, and it had nothing to do with the con. I wanted to know him better, and he didn't know me at all.

chapter sixteen

Chase insisted on walking me back to my car. It was a perfect summer's night. The air felt warm, like a soft breath on my shoulder. Tortuffo's wasn't on the beach, but it was quiet enough that I could hear the waves hitting the shore a block or so away. I was stuffed. I was lucky I hadn't exploded out of my sundress. The fritoles were amazing, like fresh warm doughnuts covered in powdered sugar with raisins and pine nuts inside. We started off with sharing one order, but ended up ordering a second plate while we talked.

I couldn't even remember everything we'd talked about. The conversation had bounced around from favorite books, to what movies we like, to what each of us thinks of ghosts (he's a believer, I'm a skeptic), to what each of us is afraid of (him heights, me spiders). The only time the conversation felt strained was when we talked about family.

Chase has two older sisters. His parents sounded pretty perfect to me, but I had the sense Chase felt he couldn't live up to his dad's expectations. It wasn't clear to me if his dad was unreasonable or if it was just the way Chase interpreted what his dad said. He, of course, wanted to know about my family, but I was pretty sure saying my mom was a maid and my dad was a convict would have brought the date to a quick close. I sort of blurred over the details, saying that my dad was self-employed (technically true—he certainly wasn't working cons for anyone else) and that my mom was in "the hotel business."

We stopped at my car, and Chase gave a low whistle before leaning over to look inside the window to see the interior.

"That is a sweet car."

"Thanks."

"And you're sure your crew won't mind helping out tomorrow?" Chase asked. Over dinner I'd volunteered to have my imaginary service organization stuff the flyers for the event. Either I was going to have to figure out how to bribe some of the waitstaff to help me or I'd be stuck doing it all myself.

"You bet." I shifted in place. I had the sense Chase was going to try to kiss me. In terms of the con, that was a big plus. It showed I was getting his trust. The downside was that I wanted him to kiss me, which meant he was becoming a distraction. I forced myself to focus on an image of Berkeley. I could meet all sorts of guys at college. There was no reason to let one attractive guy who happened to wander off to Italy to write novels, and volunteered for a children's charity, distract me from my goal.

"Can I take you for dinner again tomorrow?" Chase asked.

My mind spun around trying to figure out if I should play hard to get or agree. "You can't possibly be hungry already after that dinner," I said, buying time.

"We could take the ferry over to Seattle. I haven't been there in years."

"There's a great mystery bookstore there. It's been around forever. They always have author signings and stuff. For a mystery junkie like you, it should be heaven."

Chase's eyes lit up. "That would be awesome. If you take me there, then I'll buy you dinner as a payback. You pick the place. Maybe something seafood?"

"It's not like the store is a secret. You don't need me to find it. They have a website. One Google search and you would be good to go," I said.

Chase covered his heart with his hand. "Never. It wouldn't be the same unless you came too."

"Knowing your love for the supernatural, I have to tell you there's a ghost tour in Seattle too. It goes through the market and one of the first cemeteries and where an old brothel used to be."

"Well, now you have to clear your schedule so we can go. You can't tell a guy about books and brothels and then not take him."

I laughed. "Okay, but if we're going to fit everything in, we should go over early."

Chase looked at his watch. "When's the next ferry?"

I punched him lightly in the arm. "I was thinking something more like trying to catch the three thirty ferry tomorrow." I opened the car door. I needed to get out of there. The situation felt like it was spinning out of control. I'd planned to take some time to figure out if I should see him again, and I'd gone and thrown myself on him as his own personal Seattle tour guide.

"It seems like a long time to go without seeing you," Chase said. He brushed a lock of hair off the side of my face, and my heart sped up again. He leaned forward to kiss me.

That's when I freaked out. Not a minor freak-out either, but a full-on screaming and running in circles waving my arms kind of freak-out. Chase backed up quickly. I was fairly certain this wasn't the typical reaction he got when he tried to kiss someone. But this was an actual emergency.

"Bee!" I squealed as I ran past him flapping my arms.

"Be what?" Chase asked. He looked around trying to figure out what was causing my reaction.

I stopped a few feet away. "Is it on me?" I spun in a circle trying to see my back.

"Is what on you?"

"The bee. A bee landed on me." I looked around in case it was planning a sneak attack. "It must have been trapped in the car and flown out when I opened the door. They're not supposed to be out at night."

"I'm guessing what you're trying to say is that you're not a big fan of bees."

Now that the bee was gone, I felt like an idiot. "I'm allergic," I explained. "I break out in hives and have a hard time breathing. I haven't been stung since I was a kid, but I still can't stand them."

A group of kids ran down the street on their way to the beach. They had squirt guns and seemed to be involved in some sort of complicated military maneuver where everyone was changing sides at random. The kissing mood was over. Chase stood a respectable few feet away. I couldn't tell if he didn't want to kiss me when other people were around or if the fact that I'd acted like a total spaz had made him decide he wasn't interested in kissing me at all.

"Well, I guess I'll see you tomorrow," Chase said.

"Sure." I opened the car door wider to give any other bees a chance to make a run for it. I should have been glad he didn't kiss me. I didn't need the complication. But I couldn't help feeling disappointed. "Sorry about losing it over the bee," I said. "Logically, I know I'm bigger than they are, and if I just stood still everything would be fine, but they freak me out."

Chase chuckled. "No problem. I suppose if you're allergic, then they go from being cute little honey-makers to winged assassins."

"Exactly," I said, relieved he wasn't looking at me like I was a freak.

"I guess I lucked out. The only thing I'm allergic to is pollen. Unless I'm attacked by a flower garden, I'm pretty okay. Even if I am, the worst I have to deal with is a stuffed nose. Bee allergies are a whole different thing. You should carry one of those EpiPens."

"Is there no end to the information you know? You're also an expert on combating killer allergies?" I teased him. I didn't mention that EpiPens cost a hundred dollars if you don't have insurance, and you have to replace them every six months. I was willing to bet Chase lived in a world where everyone had insurance. Heck, his insurance would likely cover a full-time ninja nurse to follow you around with the EpiPen. She could leap from a tree and stab you with the lifesaving pen before you even knew she was there.

"I only know about it because of the McKennas. Their daughter, Ava, was allergic to bees."

chapter seventeen

I couldn't stop thinking about it. I lay in Ms. Flick's lawn chair with my hand resting on the head of one of her gnomes. The cap on the statue fit perfectly inside my hand. It was getting cool outside, but the inside of the trailer would still be hot, and I didn't want to go in. I had a fan in my room, but it didn't seem to do much to cool anything down. Instead, it made me feel like I was in a convection oven, slowly being cooked by the hot air swirling around. I wouldn't be able to sleep. There was no point in lying in bed making the sheets damp with sweat.

I shifted on the chair. It wasn't the heat that was keeping me awake. I was annoyed with myself, but I couldn't stop thinking about it. It was like having a sore tooth where you can't stop jabbing at it with your tongue despite the sharp pain. You would do it, wince at the pain, and vow to never do it again. Then you would find yourself having to do it one more time.

The idea was so absurd it was ridiculous. Yes, I looked like the picture. Sure, there were no pictures of me around from before I was three. Fine, I had a stuffed bunny, and I also had a bee allergy. But the idea that I might actually be Ava McKenna was insane. Wasn't it?

I closed my eyes and tried to remember my earliest memory. I could remember being a kid lying under a scrawny Christmas tree, chatting to it. I'd fully believed that when the holidays were over, the tree would shake off the lights and ornaments like a dog after a bath. Then it would lift up its lower branches like a long heavy skirt and walk back into the forest, where it would rejoin its extended tree family. When Christmas was over, my dad shoved the tree into a chipper behind the Save-on-Food Mart. I had howled in pain, as if he were tossing me in feet first instead of the tree. I searched my brain trying to recall how old I must have been at the time. Could I have been less than three? Then another piece of the memory slid into place. I had been inconsolable at the tree chipper, and unable to explain how I felt the tree had been murdered. The only person who had been able to make me feel better was Miss Klee, my kindergarten teacher, who just happened to be doing her shopping at the time of the tree slaughter. So I must have been at least five. Even if I were advanced for my age, I wouldn't have been allowed in kindergarten at two.

The problem with so many of my early memories was that I couldn't recall if they were really mine or simply stories I'd heard growing up. I stared up at the stars and tried to tell if I had any memories of a nanny or being taken from my family. If I had been kidnapped, it would have been traumatic. Even at three, you would think that would be something that I would remember. If I could remember being devastated at the loss of a Christmas tree, it seemed the loss of my parents would have burned some sort of memory into my head, but there was nothing about that.

Then there was the fact that I could conceive of no reason that my parents would have kidnapped anyone. There was no doubt in my mind that my dad was a crook, but he wasn't the kind of person who would harm a kid. It sounds absurd to say that he had a code of honor, but there was a sense that there were some crimes that were okay and others that were strictly off-limits. He always talked about how people might say he had no shame, but he'd never once conned an elderly person out of their money. My dad had a Robin Hood fantasy where he stole from the rich and gave to the poor. Of course, by "the poor," my dad meant himself. Still, I had a hard time imagining him sneaking into the hotel to take a toddler.

As much as it didn't make sense, I couldn't stop thinking about the possibility. My entire life would be different if I was Ava. Every kid dreams at some point about discovering that their "real" family has been found and is coming to take them away, but this felt close to being real. I was sure if I'd grown up as Ava, I'd still have problems, but from where I was sitting now, having that other life seemed magical. I could picture what my Ava room would look like: large, pink, with a giant canopy bed. I'd always wanted one of those as a kid. There would be a giant window seat with one of those custom cushions so I could sit there for hours and read. I would have traveled; I might even have a favorite place that I liked to stay when I was in Paris. I'd know where to get the best ice cream in New York City. Scrambling to find money for college wouldn't be an issue. Heck, if I really was Ava McKenna, my parents could buy me my own dorm. One thing was for sure, if I was Ava, I wouldn't have to worry that my college money had been used to get my dad out of jail.

I sat up. That was something I could check. My dad had spent more time in jail than out since I was a kid. If he was in jail when the kidnapping happened, there was no way he could have been involved.

The screen door screeched when I opened it, and I flinched. I paused in the door to see if my mom would come out, but the house stayed silent. My mom had left the light above the stove on so there was enough light to see by.

We didn't have a library or office since one of the other problems with a trailer is a serious lack of square footage. On the upside, there are a limited number of places where things can be filed away. My mom had a Rubbermaid file container she kept behind my dad's worn La-Z-Boy chair. Keeping all her important papers in one place was as far as her organizational skills went. Papers of all sorts were shoved in with no particular order. I flipped through things, trying to find anything with the raised seal of the State of Washington on it. Finally I found a copy of my dad's record. I yanked it out and carried it into the kitchen so I could read it in the light.

My finger ran down the list until the date jumped out at me. My dad had been released from jail just a few days before Ava's abduction. I swallowed. I wasn't sure what that meant. On one hand, it felt creepy, the timing too coincidental. On the other hand, I couldn't fathom that my dad would have had time to plan a kidnapping right after getting out of jail, and for some reason I couldn't imagine my mom doing it on her own.

I heard a footstep in the hall and shoved the paper in the closest drawer.

"Hey, sorry if I woke you up," I said softly. "I wanted to get a drink of water before bed."

Mom was wearing a giant sleep T-shirt with a grumpy-looking cartoon bear on the front and the saying "I'm a real bear until I get my coffee." She rubbed the sleep out of her eyes. "You didn't wake me up. I planned to stay up until you got home from your date, but I must have drifted off."

"You didn't have to wait up. How much trouble could I get into? I'm on an island."

She chucked me under the chin. "I know you; you could find plenty of trouble. I wanted to stay up because I have good news." She broke into a smile. She suddenly looked at least fifteen years younger.

I knew what she was going to say and braced myself for the news.

"Your dad is getting released!" She rose up on her tiptoes with excitement. "The paperwork will all be filed tomorrow. With luck, he'll be out of that place by the end of the week at the latest. There's a chance he could even be out tomorrow."

"That's great." I tried to sound happy, because I knew it was important to her. It wasn't that I didn't want my dad around, but I knew the trailer was going to feel a lot smaller once he arrived.

Mom hugged me. She smelled like toothpaste and the lotion she smeared on her face before bed. "It's better than great. I know you two butt heads sometimes, but that's because you're just like him. The two of you are two peas in a pod."

I didn't say anything. I hugged her back. I didn't think I was anything like my dad, and now wasn't the time to mention that I wasn't sure I was even their daughter at all.

chapter eighteen

I swapped shifts with another waitress so I could have my afternoon and evening free to go into Seattle with Chase. I usually hate working the breakfast shift. It isn't that I have anything against bacon or waffles, but people rarely order booze at breakfast. Generally I support not drinking before nine a.m., but booze drives up the check, and my tip depends on the size of the bill. However, on the plus side, I had a far better chance of avoiding running into Chase working breakfast. He didn't strike me as the kind of guy to order a giant cholesterol-laden feast first thing in the morning. He seemed more like a grab-a-muffin-and-coffee-in-the-lobby kind of guy. At least I hoped so. I had no idea how I would explain the fact I was working as a waitress if I ran into him.

The dining room was formal, with starched white napkins

and a soft loop of classical music playing in the background. Most people who came to the dining room for breakfast fell into two categories: couples who stared deeply into each other's eyes, leaving no doubt that they were simply carb loading so they would have enough energy to go back upstairs to their room and resume earlier activities, and couples who seemed to have completely run out of things to say to each other. In those cases, the man typically hid between the pages of the business section of the paper, occasionally grunting when he wanted a refill of coffee. The woman typically stared vacantly out the window, as if wishing she were anywhere but there. Families rarely ate in the formal living room, unless it was Easter or Christmas. They kept their strawberry-throwing, jam-smearing kids in the coffee shop in the lobby, which was just fine with me.

Going through the swinging door into the kitchen was like entering a portal to another world. The dishwasher, Jorge, was singing along with a Spanish radio station, and the line cooks were yelling joking insults at each other over the sounds of crashing pans and rattling dishes.

"You have my eggs benny and order of pancakes?" I yelled out.

"Coming up now," Eric said. He flipped his spatula up in the air and caught it behind his back, showing off.

"Nice moves," I said.

Chuck snorted. "It might be impressive if you did it with a knife. You don't exactly get James Bond points for doing it with a spatula. My grandma can do it with a spatula."

"That's 'cause your grandma likes to get her freak on," Eric called back. He slid two plates across the pass at me. "One stack of Vermont and two hens on a Brit."

I grabbed the plates and left the two cooks to debate the morals of each other's grandparents. I balanced the tray out into the dining room, and delivered to one of the non-talking couples. The man didn't even look up when I slid his eggs Benedict in front of him. The woman looked down at the pancakes with distrust.

"Are these the same pancakes from the menu?"

What did she think, that they were pancakes from a diner in Seattle? "Yes, ma'am. Those are our lemon ricotta pancakes. You have your choice of the fresh blueberry compote or the warm maple syrup."

"I thought they would come with fruit." She poked the pancakes with her fork. I wondered if there was any way to politely inform her that blueberries are a fruit.

"Would you like a mixed fruit side plate?" I offered.

"I suppose there's an extra charge for that," she said. When she saw me nod, she sighed deeply, as if she had to cope with a tremendous hardship. The basic room in the Keppler costs at least $250 a night. You would think that having to spring a few extra bucks for some fruit wouldn't be an issue.

I saw out of the corner of my eye that someone else had been seated in my section. That was good. I was starting to suspect that the blueberry-isn't-a-fruit lady was going to be stingy with the tip. The new couple was the exact opposite; they had pulled their chairs next to each other so they were touching. She was practically in his lap, and her hand kept running up and down his back, playing his spinal column like a keyboard.

I grabbed a fresh silver carafe of coffee and two of the menus. "Good morning. Welcome to the—" My voice froze shut in my throat when they turned to face me. It was Brendan and Blow Job Becky.

Brendan's shirt was rumpled. No doubt he had picked it up off the floor just moments ago. Rebecca had pulled her hair back into a ponytail, and managed to put on some lip gloss and mascara, but there was no mistaking that fresh-out-of-bed look.

Rebecca giggled and wound her hand into Brendan's hair. "Well, this is awkward," she said.

"No reason for things to be awkward. Sadie and I aren't a couple. There's not a thing between us, is there?" Brendan said with a pointed look.

I pressed my mouth into what I hoped passed for a smile. "Nope. Not a thing. You guys make a great couple." I left off the part that I was well aware that since Rebecca had pretty much slept with everyone else, that it was merely a matter of time until she worked her way back around to Brendan for a second try. This time it looked like she was hoping to make it more than a one-night kind of thing. Not that I cared what either of them did.

"I think it's sweet you guys have been friends for so long," Rebecca said, trailing her hand along Brendan's back.

I felt my nostrils flare out in annoyance. Brendan wasn't saying anything more, but there was a hint of a smirk on his face. Why couldn't they sleep together in a car like every other high school student? No doubt Brendan let Rebecca pay for a room here because he wanted me to either see them or hear about it from one of my coworkers. "Would you like some coffee?" I managed to get out.

"I don't *want* coffee, I need it." Rebecca pushed her coffee cup toward me. I filled the cup and then paused over Brendan's.

"Do you need it too?" I asked.

"Nah, I just want it."

I managed to avoid gagging, filled his cup, and dropped off the menus. I shoved the kitchen door open and went straight to the fridge. I acted like I needed to get butter or cream, but the truth was, I just wanted to be someplace cool and alone. I wondered if I could stay there until the end of my shift.

"You okay?" Libby asked, sticking her head in the walk-in. Libby had been a waitress at the hotel for fifteen years.

"Did you see the lovebirds?" I asked.

"You know the only reason he's with her is to bug you. The boy is crazy about you. He's doing this to get your attention. And no matter what they're playing at, they weren't here together last night."

I snorted. "Are you kidding me? Did you see them out there?"

“I heard them talking when they came in. They met up in the lobby to come for breakfast.”

I hated that my heart sped up a bit at the idea that they hadn’t been together. I shrugged nonchalantly. “It doesn’t matter to me. He can be with whoever he wants, but I would think he could do better than her.” I left off the part where anyone could do better than her; you could date a petri dish of the bubonic plague and still be ahead.

“You want me to take their table? It looks like all you have left is those two and the old couple in the corner. I can take them both if you want, and you can scoot out of here.”

I felt a million pounds lighter, as if I could take my first deep breath. “Are you sure?” I was already untying my apron.

“Sure. It’s summer. There must be something you’d rather be doing.”

“Thanks, Libby. You’ve earned yourself valuable karma points.”

She waved me off. “Yeah, yeah. Get out of here.”

I slid out through the back of the kitchen and quickly changed into the clothes I’d stuck in the staff break room. I shoved my uniform into my bag. I needed to pick up the boxes of flyers and programs for the fund-raiser. If I wanted to get it done before the afternoon ferry, I was going to have to get busy.

The hotel’s back passageway runs from the storage room to the ballrooms, and makes it easier to move furniture without disrupting guests. Along the walls are framed photos of the staff.

There was a giant staff party at the beginning of each summer. I think the idea is that free BBQ, lemonade, and three-legged races for the kids should make up for the low pay and long hours. And it seems to work; people love it. As I raced down the hall, one of the photos caught my eye.

I backed up a step and pulled the frame off the wall so I could see it more clearly. Brendan's mom and dad were in the foreground. In her arms was a small toddler that had to be Brendan. I searched the crowd and spotted my mom. She didn't have me with her. I walked back down the hall and searched each of the photos. I finally found one where I was in the shot. I had to be at least four.

"Hey there," a voice said.

I jumped as if I'd been spotted doing something wrong. It was Thomas.

"Your mom caught me yesterday in the hall and said you might not be heading off in the fall and were looking to stay on staff," Thomas said.

"My mom's confused. There have been a few hiccups, but I'm still going to college. I'm not planning on staying," I clarified. "You know how moms are. They never want you to leave home."

Thomas laughed. "Could be worse. She could be pushing you out the door. If something changes, you let me know. You're a good worker. You're always welcome here, even if you just want to work during Christmas and summer holidays."

I motioned to the frames. "Based on all the photos, this place is practically my second home."

"All part of the Keppler happy family."

I bit my lip. "Hey, Thomas, you know what's weird? I don't see any pictures of me when I was little. The other staff have their kids in the pictures. What was I, some kind of hellion? Maybe a vampire, no one could get me on film?"

"Course you're in the pictures." Thomas motioned to the photo of me when I was about five.

"I don't see any where I'm younger, like really little."

Thomas shifted his weight and his eyes slid away from mine. "Oh, I'm sure there are some shots around here."

"I looked."

"Well, they can't hang up all the pictures. There are probably some stuck away in a cupboard somewhere." Thomas held up his clipboard as if he was suddenly reminded that there was someplace he was supposed to be.

"Where would they be? I'd like to look through them." It wasn't all in my head; Thomas still wouldn't meet my eyes. There was something he didn't want me to know.

"Ah, heck, I don't know. You don't want to look through a bunch of dusty old pictures. There has to be something more fun you could be doing with your time."

"See, the thing is, my mom just found out a while ago that all my baby pictures got ruined. I'd love to find a picture of me when I was little that I could give to my mom."

Thomas looked up. He looked like a deer in the headlights. "Oh. I'll look around when I get a chance. I might be able to dig up a photo." He glanced down at his wrist. "I should get going."

"Sure." I watched Thomas as he walked away quickly in the other direction. It wasn't my imagination. He was nervous. Now if I could only figure out what to do with my suspicions.

chapter nineteen

"I want to see the place where they toss the fish," Chase said.

We rounded the corner at First Street, and Chase nearly bounced up and down when he caught sight of the red neon Pike Place Market sign.

"You know, we don't have to fit all of the Seattle tourist sites into one visit," I pointed out. We'd already stopped at the Mystery Bookshop and strolled through Pioneer Square.

Chase grabbed my hand, and we wound our way through the thick crowd of tourists that always surrounded the fish shop. The clerk, dressed in his orange rubber waders, called out the order for salmon, and another clerk chucked the giant silver fish through the air. Flashes went off as the groups of tourists tried to capture the moment on film. The first clerk caught the fish and the crowd let out an appreciative whoop.

I dragged Chase away from the crowd to a small store wedged in the corner. The brass bell rang as we entered. The store walls had shelves from top to bottom filled with giant glass mason jars full of spices and teas. Chase paused inside the door and took a deep breath. His face split into a smile.

"This place reminds me of something out of a Harry Potter book," I confessed.

Chase wandered along the wall, reading the tags for the jars. "I wouldn't be at all surprised if they had eye of newt in this place," he said.

I smiled. It felt like Chase had passed some sort of test by liking the store. A test I didn't even know I was giving him. "Come on. I have a lot I want to show you before the market closes."

I pointed out all the sights while we wandered. The original Starbucks; the flower stalls; the place that made every possible type of pasta, including a chocolate fettuccine; the vegetable stalls stacked with red peppers, giant leeks, and quirky things you hardly ever see, like purple potatoes.

The market merchants were starting to wrap up for the day, either piling things into giant Rubbermaid containers or covering the stalls with bright blue tarps. Chase left me rifling through a stack of woven scarves while he went to take a picture. When I spun around, he was standing there with a giant bouquet of flowers. It was practically a bush of bright, candy-colored flowers. I almost fell into the scarf booth.

"Flowers for the lady." Chase bent over gallantly and passed me the bouquet.

"Are you crazy? These must have cost a fortune." My hand barely fit around the wrapped stems.

"They gave me a deal because it's the end of the day. Besides, it's the least I can do since you're showing me all around the city. And don't forget you got your team to do all those brochures this afternoon. I'll have to thank them, too."

I had folded and stuffed five hundred programs all by myself. My paper cuts had paper cuts. "Everyone was glad to help," I lied. "It's a great cause."

I looked down at the bouquet. I couldn't recall anyone ever getting me flowers before. I didn't even know if my family owned a vase. Everything Chase said and did seemed like a glimpse into an alien world. An intoxicating, wonderful world. A place where people traveled, and gentlemen opened the door for you, and brought flowers instead of a six-pack of beer.

"The communications director for the foundation is coming tomorrow. You should bring all the volunteers by. We could take a picture for our newsletter."

My imaginary community service group was becoming a hassle. "I'll try, but you know how it is getting people together in the summer. I'm surprised the director is coming over already. The event isn't until this weekend."

Chase rolled his eyes. "We've hit a snag. Remember how I was telling you that the McKenna family isn't that crazy about Nancy Goodall, their old nanny?"

I nodded.

"She announced on her new TV show last night that she's attending the event. Near as we can tell, she doesn't have tickets to the fund-raiser, but the hotel confirmed she just made a reservation."

"She has to know they wouldn't want her there. Why is she showing up?"

He shrugged. "Your guess is as good as mine. The communications director is afraid she's going to be dragging a bunch of camera people with her and doing a segment for her new show, trying to profit off all the media attention the event is getting. As far as the McKennas are concerned, there's nothing she wouldn't do for some extra time in the spotlight. They don't want her to capitalize further on the death of their daughter."

I used the tip of my shoe to outline one of the cobblestones. "Are the McKennas certain their daughter is dead?"

"I think at this point they've acknowledged that's the most likely outcome. Mr. McKenna wanted for years to purchase a headstone for Ava to put in the family plot. Mrs. McKenna has always refused, but I heard from my parents they've gone ahead and ordered one."

"Do you know why they never had more kids?" I asked. I took another deep sniff of the bouquet, before forcing myself to focus on what Chase could tell me.

Chase looked down the street while he thought. "I think at

first they couldn't face the idea of having a kid around. They didn't want to feel like they were replacing Ava. Then Mrs. McKenna got really involved with the foundation, and he got busy with his company." He shrugged. "It's like there was this window of opportunity for them to be parents, and they missed it."

"What kind of parents do you think they would have been?" I found myself holding my breath while he answered. I mentally kicked myself. These questions had nothing to do with the con. At some level I was still enjoying the fantasy that they were my secret family, and it, along with my fantasies involving Chase, were distracting me from my job.

"Mrs. McKenna loves kids. She's one of those people who never talks down to them. You can tell that she's actually interested in what they have to say. When she's around kids for a foundation fund-raiser, she's always the one who plops onto the floor to play a game, and never freaks out if one of the kids touches her with paint on their hands."

"What about him?"

Chase laughed, and it struck me how model perfect he was. Even his teeth were attractive. "Here's a secret you can never tell my mom when you meet her. When I was in high school, I got busted at this party. Someone's parents were out of town, and we'd pretty much trashed the place. I guess one of the neighbors called the cops. When the police showed up, I was puking in the front hall planter."

"Classy."

"That was me, classy. I was terrified to call my folks, because I knew they would kill me. My mom's dad was an alcoholic, so she's supersensitive about any kind of drinking, not to mention I'd lied to them and told them I was sleeping at a friend's house. So instead of calling them, I called Mr. McKenna. He was in town for business so I called his hotel. Just imagine what he must have thought, getting this call from his friend's kid. It's one thirty in the morning, I'm drunk, I might even have been crying because I was freaking out about the cops, so it's not exactly the kind of call everyone wants to get."

"What did he do?" Chase's story fascinated me. I'd never worried much about my parents being mad at me. My mom just ignored any information she didn't want to know, and my dad didn't seem to care what I did. The closest I'd come to this kind of trouble was last summer, when I'd taken some rum my dad had to a party at the beach. My dad wasn't mad that I'd been drinking; he was mad I'd taken his rum.

"Mr. McKenna showed up at the party. The police wouldn't let anyone leave except with an adult, so he agreed to take responsibility for me. I remember he had these plaid pajamas on under his trench coat. He took me back to the hotel. He made me take a shower to clean up. He sent my puked-on sweatshirt down to be cleaned and ordered up some food from room service. I slept on the sofa in his room that night and he took me home in the morning. I was sure he was going to come in and tell my parents what an idiot I was, but he didn't. He stopped the car down the block and told me to remember that people are a sum of the decisions they make, and making stupid decisions is part of growing up, but not learning from them means you're stupid."

"That was the end of the lecture?"

"Short and sweet. The thing is, that lecture stuck with me. It was up to me to decide what kind of person I wanted to be, and I didn't want to be the kind of person who's known for puking in planters."

"It's not that simple though, is it? I mean, people aren't shaped just by their choices. So many of our possible choices are set by the time we're born. Who your parents are and what you have growing up makes a huge difference," I pointed out.

"I don't believe that. I mean, it might be harder to make good choices if you don't come from a stable home where people are around to model that behavior for you, but ultimately it's up to each person."

I considered debating the issue with Chase. People who think you can be all you can be by pulling up your bootstraps are typically people who never had to worry about having boots to start with.

"Of course everyone is responsible for their own actions, but some people have reasons for why their lives are a mess," I tried to explain.

"They're a mess because they aren't trying hard enough. People complain about not having enough, but it's because they don't make their own opportunities."

I felt like chucking the bouquet at him. The lights in the market were starting to go out as vendors finished packing up for the night. It felt like dark clouds were moving in. I could just imagine what Chase would think of someone like my dad, or Brendan, or, for that matter, me. What would he make of the opportunities my family had seized?

"What do you say we grab some dinner?" Chase was smiling at me. Of course, he was actually smiling at someone he thought was a carefree college-bound girl who came from an upstanding family in the community and volunteered her time for charity events. The kind of girl I might have been if I'd grown up with people like the McKennas as parents. If Chase knew the real me, he would grab his flowers back with a look of disgust and run the opposite direction.

"Sure, there's a seafood place a few blocks from here." I turned to lead the way. The street angled sharply uphill.

Chase lightly touched my elbow. "Hey, you okay? You look sad all of a sudden."

He had no clue. "I was just thinking about the McKenna family. Maybe Ava is still out there somewhere. Maybe there's still a chance for her to come home."

"I had no idea you were such a hopeful person," Chase said.

"Sometimes hope is all you've got."

chapter twenty

Chase and I took the last ferry home at midnight and then stayed up until two a.m. sitting on the beach and talking. I didn't regret a moment of it until my alarm went off at five a.m. for breakfast service. Three hours does not count as a night of sleep. It's more of a long nap. I thought about calling in sick, but it would have left Libby in the lurch, and after she'd let me bail yesterday, I couldn't do that to her.

My tips were lousy. I practically paid *them* for the pleasure of working. It was my own fault. I dropped a plate of scrambled eggs into one woman's lap. I screwed up a bunch of orders and gave a cheese omelet to a guy who was lactose intolerant. The killer was that I kept forgetting to refill people's coffee. Denying people access to caffeine first thing in the morning is a surefire way to make sure they leave you only a single dollar and complain to the manager. All I wanted to do was go home, peel off my uniform, and crawl back into bed, but as soon as I pulled into my driveway, it became apparent that bed wasn't going to happen.

I parked my scooter. If I'd made a list of people who I didn't want to see today, the two sitting across from each other at the picnic table would have been at the top of it. Although both of them must have heard me approach, neither bothered to look up from the deck of cards on the table.

"Can you see it?" my dad asked. His voice sounded like he smoked four or five packs of cigarettes a day, but he actually didn't smoke at all.

Brendan fanned out the cards, then gathered them up and tapped each side of the deck on the table before picking a card at random and inspecting the back. "I give. Did you use some kind of ink to mark them? Maybe something that only shows up with a blue light or something?" He tilted the deck of cards into the sun.

My dad barked out a laugh. "Where am I going to hide a blue light at a poker game? Nah, I shaved the deck." He took the cards from Brendan, sorted them, and then ran his thumb along the side. "There. Try feeling it now."

I stood next to the picnic table with my arms crossed. Shaving cards, usually done with superfine sandpaper, is a classic way to mark the cards. If you have the touch, you can feel the difference between the cards and cut the deck so you always came up with a winning hand. Magicians use shaved and marked cards to pull off their tricks. Cons use them to ensure they always have the luck. Of course, if someone catches you cheating, they might finish the game by beating you up in an alley, which feels a lot less lucky. My dad wasn't the best con artist, but I will give him credit for being good with cards. I couldn't remember a time when he didn't have a pack in his hands or in a pocket.

Brendan ran the ball of his thumb against the deck. He pulled a card out and flipped it over. A four of diamonds. He cursed and my dad laughed.

"You gotta have the touch. Featherlight," Dad said, waggling his fingers in Brendan's face. "I worked on this deck for weeks. It's a thing of beauty. It's like Michelangelo himself shaved this deck. I can feel it, but no one else is going to notice a thing."

I picked up the deck and felt the sides of the cards. I quickly fanned through the facedown deck and picked out four cards. I looked down at them and smiled, then tossed the four aces faceup on the table.

My dad scowled and scooped up the cards. His complexion had the gray pasty color that comes from being locked up. He had also gained weight, his skin looking puffy on his frame. Prison food is heavy on the carbs, low on nutritional value.

"Welcome home," I said.

My dad grunted, which I took to mean, *"Thank you, daughter. I am glad to be back home in the bosom of my family. While in prison I realized that we were never as close as we should have been, and I'm going to dedicate my life to making our relationship better."* I watched him shuffle the deck, cutting then recutting it. Maybe the reason we were never close was because I wasn't really his daughter. On the other hand, if he went to all the trouble to steal a kid, you would think he would want me around. Otherwise, why not just get a puppy?

"Your mom wants to have a big family dinner tonight," Dad said. "She wanted me to tell you." He looked up at me. "She's working today. It'd be nice if you got the dinner going so she didn't have to come home and do the cooking."

I thought of pointing out that if he really wanted to do something nice, *he* could do the cooking. "I didn't know you'd be home. I made plans for dinner. Maybe you and Mom could have a nice romantic dinner with just the two of you."

"It must be that time of the year. Love is in the air," Brendan said.

I tried to freeze him in place with my eyes. "Well, you would know."

Brendan looked at my dad. "If I didn't know better, I would say she sounded jealous, which doesn't make any sense, because she's not interested in me."

"Don't even try to make sense of a woman and what comes out of her mouth." Dad and Brendan bumped fists in manly solidarity. I ground down a layer of enamel in annoyance. I couldn't fathom Chase sitting there acting like someone from a cheap beer ad talking about poker and how women are so annoying. There were people who fist bumped, and people who belonged to country clubs, and I knew which one I would prefer to be a part of.

My dad turned back to me. "You'll have to cancel your plans. Your mom is really excited about this dinner." He heaved himself up from the picnic table. "I should get going. I want to get down to the garden center."

I rolled my eyes. Ninety-nine percent of our yard looked like it had mange, with dried dirt patches and the occasional pathetic patch of grass poking up here and there. The term "green thumb" was not one that I would typically use for my dad, but for whatever reason he had a passion for the rosebush he'd planted in the far back corner of our yard. The same guy who couldn't be bothered to do anything about the sea of dandelions would carefully fluff the dirt around the rosebush so that it was as soft as a baby's blanket. He practically trimmed the bush with nail clippers. I suppose it could be worse; Brendan's dad collected vintage beer cans. I was willing to bet Chase's dad collected some kind of china figurines that used to belong to royalty.

"Brendan, you tell your dad I'll come by and see him later this week." Dad tapped his watch at me. "Six p.m. for dinner and don't make salmon or nothing. I hate the way the fish smell sticks around the house when it's hot like this. A steak would be nice."

I watched him walk away. I wanted to hurl my helmet after him. What did he think I was, the family's personal waitress?

Should I ask him how he wanted his steak cooked? Iron his napkin? He turned around and saw my expression.

"Don't make that face at me. This is for your mom. She wants a nice family dinner, so that's what she's going to get."

"Fine."

He hadn't even waited for my answer. The screen door was already slamming shut behind him.

"You know what they say: You can pick your nose, and you can pick your friends, but you can't pick your family," Brendan said.

"Thank you, Aristotle, for that piece of timeless philosophy." I chewed the inside of my lip. "The thing is, I'm starting to think they might not be my family at all. Maybe I do get to choose."

chapter twenty-one

Brendan raised an eyebrow. "Let's go for a walk." He cocked his head at the path that wove between the trailers and out back toward the fields.

"I don't have time to take a walk. I've got to go grocery shopping so I can make a nice family dinner so we can all sit around looking at each other in silence because we have nothing to say," I grumbled.

"What did you mean, they might not be your family?"

"Nothing. Forget it," I said, suddenly embarrassed that I had said anything out loud.

"You can't drop a bomb like that and tell me to forget it. Is this about the McKennas?"

I turned and shot a nervous look at the screen door. I wasn't sure if my dad could overhear us or not. I put my finger in front of my mouth, indicating that Brendan should keep his voice down. "I'm not talking about this here," I whispered.

"That's why I suggested we should take a walk," Brendan said as if he were pointing out the obvious.

There was no getting rid of Brendan when he was focused on something like this. If I went inside to avoid him, he would stand out here and talk loudly until the entire trailer park knew what was going on. "Give me two minutes; I have to change."

Brendan smiled, happy about getting his way. "I'll be right here."

When I came back outside, he was lying across the picnic bench, bopping his head to the music on his iPod. He sat up when he heard the screen door shut. He opened his mouth, and I shook my head so he would shut up and pointed toward the woods. I marched off without waiting to see if he was behind me.

"We should check to see if the blackberries are ripe," Brendan suggested, either ignoring that I was annoyed with him or completely unaware. He motioned for us to take the path that led down to the old Laughton fields. Mr. Laughton used to keep a herd of sheep there. They were long gone, but their grazing paddock was still there. The fence was mostly rotted away, although you had to be careful in places or you would trip over a section. At the far side of the field, giant wild blackberry bushes grew. As long as you were willing to sacrifice a layer or two of skin to the thorns, the berries were free for the taking.

In the shade of the woods it was at least ten degrees cooler. I lifted my hair off my neck so I could feel the cool air.

"So tell me what's up," Brendan said.

"It's stupid." I suddenly felt embarrassed to say it out loud.

"I've always listened to your stupid ideas. Why would I stop now?"

I couldn't stop a laugh from sneaking out. "You really should go into counseling with your ability to make people feel better and open up." I took a deep breath. "Don't argue with me, just listen; okay?"

Brendan nodded.

"I know this sounds crazy, but I think, I mean, I think there is a chance . . ." I stumbled, trying to find a way to put it into words without sounding delusional.

"You think you are Ava McKenna," Brendan guessed.

"I don't know. I think I *could* be." I shrugged. "There's a bunch of stuff. It isn't just that I look like the picture. I'm the right age. There's the fact that my parents have no baby pictures of me. Who doesn't have baby pictures of their only kid? My mom says it's because the trailer flooded, but she's lying about some things, and there is this whole list of odd coincidences." I counted the items off on my fingers. "I found out she was questioned by the cops when Ava went missing, but when I brought it up to her, she acted like it never happened. And it's not just her; there are no pictures of me as a kid at any of the staff events at the hotel. It's like I never existed before the age of three."

I looked over at Brendan. I couldn't read his expression. We walked in silence until I couldn't stand it any longer. "So? What do you think?"

"Stranger things have happened." Brendan shrugged. "But, if you're asking me which is more likely, that the shitter trailer you live in leaked and ruined your baby photos or that your parents kidnapped you from the McKennas, then I'm going to lean toward the leak."

"What about the fact that my mom lied about the cops talking to her?"

"Your mom isn't exactly the best at dealing with things that make her uncomfortable. Remember when you had that hamster and she told you that he ran away and was living with Santa at the North Pole? And how the hamster had his own little elf hat and shoes and apparently had a natural talent for making toys?"

"People tell their kids those kind of lies all the time. Who wants to crush their child's heart by telling them that Mr. Fuzzy is garden compost?" I said.

"Fair enough, but my point is that your mom didn't tell you the story just to make you feel better; I think she told it so *she* would feel better. I'm not even convinced she didn't believe it. So if she can convince herself that Mr. Fuzzy, who couldn't run on his wheel without falling off, could wield power tools to make toys, she could definitely delete any memories of the police talking to her."

I kicked a rock on the path and watched it skip along. "It's not that I disagree with what you're saying, and if it was just one thing, I might feel differently, but it's everything added together."

"You're not thinking it all the way through. What about everyone else?" Brendan asked.

"What do you mean?"

"This isn't exactly a major city. Wouldn't other people on the island notice that your parents suddenly had a kid? How would they explain suddenly having a toddler?"

I felt my brain screech to a stop. I hadn't thought about that. "Maybe they told people I was adopted," I said, knowing it was lame even as it came out of my mouth.

"You know I don't necessarily have a huge amount of respect for the police, but I have to think they would have been a bit suspicious if your parents suddenly adopted a kid the same age and general appearance of a kid that had just gone missing. It's not exactly a case that requires Sherlock Holmes to solve."

I started walking faster. I was mad at myself for not thinking of how my parents would have had to explain things. I felt stupid, and I hate feeling stupid. I wished I hadn't said anything to Brendan. If I had kept it to myself, I could still hold on to the secret dream that I was Ava. Part of me always knew that it wasn't really possible. I wasn't going to wake up and discover I had this amazing life, but I had really liked imagining what it would have been like.

"Are you pissed?" Brendan asked, trailing after me.

"No."

He laughed. "You're totally pissed. You should see your face. You asked me what I thought. You should know not to ask me if you don't want to know the truth."

"I'm not mad about that," I lied.

"So, you're just randomly annoyed?"

I stopped short and Brendan almost ran into me. "I have plenty to be annoyed about," I said. "What about the thing with you and Rebecca? Are you going to look me in the eye and tell me you suddenly discovered you had feelings for her? Because I'm pretty sure the only reason you slept with her was to annoy me." I crossed my arms over my chest and waited to see what he said.

"Yeah. Pretty much. I mean, I'd also sleep with her because I'm a guy and she was offering, but the main goal would be to tick you off."

I stared at him with my mouth open. "You're disgusting. So you're admitting that you did sleep with her. I knew it."

Brendan cocked his head. "Now, if I didn't know better, I would say it matters to you if I slept with her or not."

"I don't care."

"Yeah, you do." Brendan smiled. "If it makes you feel better, I didn't sleep with her."

I looked into his face. "Really?"

Brendan's smile widened triumphantly. "So you do care."

I wanted to scream. "Do whatever you want. Do *whomever* you want. It's your life; feel free to screw it up any way you want."

"At least I know who I am."

"What does that mean?"

"You talk about how your mom doesn't always like to face real life, but you do the same thing. You decided that your real life doesn't measure up, so it isn't going to even count until you can run away and pretend to be someone else. No wonder you were excited about the idea of being Ava McKenna. It's a dream come true. You don't have to make up a better life; you had one all along before it was taken away from you."

"That's not true," I stammered.

"Look, I know I can be an asshole sometimes. I take the easy way out and I don't try hard enough on things that don't come easily to me. I'm sarcastic and arrogant. I'm not good about talking about my feelings. I'm not stupid, but I'm not book smart, I never got algebra, and when we had to read Shakespeare, I couldn't figure out what the hell he was saying half the time."

"What's the point of this? Do you want me to tell you, 'Oh no, that's not true, you're a great guy'?" I said.

"No. I don't need you to tell me. All those negative things I said? Those are true. You know what else is true? I'm funny; I can make people laugh. I'm willing to take risks and go after what I want. I'm street smart and I can read people. There is nothing I wouldn't do for the people I love." Brendan threw his arms up in the air. "Don't you get it? I like who I am. Who I really am. Not who I wish I was, or who I plan to be someday. And for the record, I like you, too, even if you don't."

"I like myself," I said quietly.

"Then why do you keep trying to run away? Don't you get that even if you were the missing princess Ava, you would still be you?"

"This isn't about wanting to be a princess." I wanted to yell in frustration. "Haven't you ever felt like this isn't your real life? That this can't be it. That something good, something amazing, has to happen, because if you wake up thirty years from now and realize that you still live in a shitty trailer, and work as a greeter at Walmart, and the highlight of your day is getting cheese half off at the grocery because it's close to its expiration date, you will start screaming and not be able to stop."

"You know what would be worse? Waking up thirty years from now and realizing you've missed your whole life because you were waiting for a chance to be someone different."

"That's not what I'm doing."

Brendan shook his head, clearly not convinced. "I stopped by today because I have some news. Nanny Goodall is coming here."

"How did you know that?" I asked. I couldn't imagine that Chase would have mentioned anything to Brendan, although the idea of the two of them somehow talking without me being around to supervise made me very nervous.

Brendan wriggled his eyebrows. "I invited her."

I felt my heart speed up. "What do you mean, you invited her?"

"I called her office and hinted at what we knew. I suggested that if she wanted to keep things a secret, she would show up here." He spread his arms like I should leap into them as a thank-you.

"Why did you do that?"

"Because the whole point of this is to pull a con that gets you enough money to go to school." Brendan looked around as if the trees might call out another answer. "That's what we set out to do, isn't it? I thought you would be happy. Any doubt that she lied about something disappeared the second I had her on the phone. She was very interested in what I had to say. She was the one who said, and I'm quoting here, 'Perhaps there is a way to make it worth your while to avoid dragging the whole situation up.' *Worth my while.* I could practically hear her pulling out her checkbook on the phone."

My mind tried to process what he was saying. "I know I asked you to help, but that doesn't mean that I wanted you going off and calling people without talking to me. Chase told me that the McKenna family feels that she used their tragedy to be some big media whore. He said they're really upset that she's coming."

"I thought we covered the fact that the McKennas aren't your long-lost real family."

"It doesn't mean that I want anyone to get hurt."

"Are you kidding me? It's not like I'm hooking their body parts up to a car battery. They don't even have to talk to her." Brendan ran his hands through his hair. "You asked me to help you with this. Now you're pissed because I did. I don't get it. I don't get you at all. You were the one who wanted to be with me, and then when we slept together, you started avoiding me. Then you tell me that you don't want to be with me and that I should move on, and when you think I'm hooking up with Rebecca, you're ticked. You ask me for my opinion on your princess fantasy, and when I give it to you, you're angry with that. I don't know what the hell you want anymore."

"I don't know either," I said softly.

"Tell you what, call me when you figure it out." Brendan turned around and headed back the way we came. He got a few feet away and stopped. "Goodall is coming in a couple days. She's prepared to pay up. You want to go to California, you want to have your life do-over, then she's your chance." He didn't wait to hear what I might say. He spun around and walked away.

chapter twenty-two

My dad stood over the grill, supervising the steaks. He was wearing my mom's apron with the outline of a woman's body in a pink bikini on the front. My mom had insisted on a tablecloth for the picnic table and was pouring glasses of iced tea for her and me. My dad was already on his third beer. He looked out over the yard like he was king of the castle. A trailer castle.

It would have been easier for my dad if we had moved a lot. Most con artists move towns frequently to avoid being known by the local cops, but for whatever reason my dad wanted to stay here and put down roots. Well, as rooted as you can be when your house has no foundation.

"How do you want your steak?" Dad asked when I came out carrying the potato salad and a stack of napkins.

"Medium rare," I said.

He wrinkled up his face. "How can you eat that? Pretty soon you'll tell me you like your steak still mooing. If you're going to eat meat, make sure it's dead first. I'll cook it well done like your mom's and mine."

I slid the potato salad onto the table. I had no idea why he bothered to ask me what I wanted if he wasn't interested in the answer.

Mom looked down at the table. "Oh, Sadie, can you put the salad in a serving dish? It's so much nicer that way."

I glanced down at the plastic tub of salad I'd picked up from the grocery store. "If I stick it in another dish, it's just going to be more to wash up later," I pointed out. "I didn't think we were exactly going for Buckingham Palace standards."

"Your mom wants a serving dish, get her a dish," Dad instructed in a don't-argue-with-me voice. "And bring me back another beer." He looked at my mom. "And a glass." He tapped his deck of cards on the side of the grill and flipped over the top card. "Queen of hearts. I should have known."

My mom giggled. Parents could be disgusting. I ignored them and went back inside to get the dish, a beer, *and* a glass. Of course they didn't care: I was going to be the one stuck doing the dishes later.

My phone was sitting on the kitchen counter. I took a quick peek. There was another call from Chase. He'd left a few messages. I didn't want to call him back until I'd figured out what to do. I didn't need any other information from him to make the con work. Goodall was already on her way. The only reason to stay in touch with him was because I liked him. And what was the point? He didn't know the real me, and if he did, he wouldn't be interested. It wasn't exactly a relationship with a big future. It sounded perfectly logical, but it didn't change how I felt. I wanted to call him back because I liked him. As much as I wanted to pretend it was just about the con, I knew that wasn't true. I needed to figure out either how to use the information on Goodall or how to get him to like the real me before I called.

Brendan hadn't called. My fingers ran over the keypad. I could call him, but I wasn't sure what to say to him, either. No wonder Brendan didn't think I was making any sense lately. I couldn't figure out what I was doing, let alone how to explain it to anyone else.

"Dinner's on!" Dad called out. "That beer isn't getting any colder, so you might as well bring it out."

When I sat back at the picnic table, I could tell my dad had cooked the steaks past well done and into charcoaled shoe leather territory. I pushed mine around on my plate, hoping if I coated it with steak sauce it might be moist enough to be swallowed without sucking all the saliva out of my throat. What a shame we didn't do more of these family dinners. I'd forgotten how much fun they could be.

"Eat up," Dad said. "We don't want leftovers if we're leaving."

I dropped my fork. "What do you mean, leaving?"

My mom lightly punched my dad in the shoulder. "It was

supposed to be a surprise. I thought we'd take a family vacation this weekend, pop up to Lake Roosevelt. They have that Coulee Dam there, and your dad can do some fishing while you and I sit on the beach and soak up some sun." My mom was as excited as if we were planning a posh European vacation instead of planning to sleep in a tent being consumed by mosquitoes. She and I had completely different ideas of fun.

"I can't lie in the sun. I burn," I reminded her. Both of my parents are the kind of people who turn a nice golden brown in the time it takes them to walk from the trailer to the car. I, on the other hand, am the kind of person who tends to turn bright lobster red unless I slather myself with SPF sixty million.

"My first plan was Portland, but your dad isn't allowed to leave the state."

"The probation officer I pulled this time is a real dick. He'll only let me take the weekend as a break, and then I'm supposed to be doing a job search." Dad shook his head as if he couldn't believe the injustice of the justice system.

"I guess he figures you've sort of had a two-year break already," I said. My dad and regular employment were not very well acquainted. "I can't go away this weekend. I've got plans." My mom's face fell and I could see my dad's expression starting to harden. "I promised to work that big party at the hotel," I lied. "I can't back out on Thomas." I wasn't sure if I wanted to go through with the scam on the nanny, but I at least wanted to stay in town so I had the option. Chase would also leave town after this weekend. I wasn't prepared to accept the idea of never seeing him again. I might not have any idea how we would make a real relationship work, but that didn't mean I was ready to give up on the idea. "Maybe we could go some other time," I suggested. Some other time, like after I was enrolled in school and living far away.

My dad shifted in his seat. "I don't want to be around this weekend."

"You could go without me," I offered.

"If the whole family doesn't go, it doesn't much count as a family vacation," my mom pointed out. "We could go next weekend, I guess."

"I really didn't want to stick around this weekend with all those people arriving," my dad grumbled. "Stan was telling me on the ferry that a bunch of TV types have already started arriving. The whole place is going to be thick with them."

I raised an eyebrow. It wasn't like my dad tended to hang out at the hotel beach, where he would have to jockey for a place to lay his towel. Not to mention I didn't think the media was going to be hounding him for an interview. "I'm looking forward to it. They say some celebrities might show up. I think it will be fun."

"You always did love a party," Mom said. "I remember how excited you were for your first birthday. You were crazy for that Dora the Explorer. When she would come on the TV, you would squeal. We did a whole Dora-themed party. Do you remember that?" she asked.

"No." I couldn't recall having any interest in Dora, let alone a full-on girl crush on her.

"We had paper hats and paper plates with her face on it. Your dad made sure we ordered a giant sheet cake that had Dora and . . . what was that monkey's name?"

"Can't say I recall," my dad said, scratching his chin with his beer.

"Something Hispanic, I think. Diego, maybe? Or was that the name of her other friend?" I could see my mom searching her mental database for the lost monkey name. "I remember that he wore those giant red boots. So we stuck that sheet cake down in front of you, and before I could snap a picture, you slammed your hands right down on that cake. I think you wanted to hug Dora."

"That, or she hated the monkey," my dad suggested.

Mom laughed. "You smeared that frosting all over everything. You had it in your hair and nose. I think I found some cleaning out your ears like a day or two later. I can't believe you don't remember that."

"I was only one." The more my mom talked about the party, the more nervous it made me. It was too Disney Technicolor perfect. "Do you remember that party, Dad?"

He jumped slightly and his eyes slid away from mine. "Not sure."

"It was my first birthday, and it sounds like Mom threw quite the party," I said. Mom was nodding at him.

"Course I remember. Frosting everywhere." He looked down

at his steak and then attacked it with his knife and fork as if he was afraid it might be about to make a run for it. The poor thing had already been cremated; I couldn't imagine the steak had any chance of getting away.

I looked around the table in search of an excuse to leave. I seized my mom's iced tea glass. "Let me get you some more."

I slammed the screen door behind me and scooped up my phone. I typed Dora the Explorer into the search engine and pulled up the Wikipedia link. All I needed were the basics. First off, the monkey's name was Boots. Secondly, Dora first went on the air several years after I was born. No way I had a Dora-themed first birthday unless I was psychic. No Dora, no Boots the monkey, and no frosting in my nose. The whole thing was a lie. My mom tended to make up stories when she didn't like the truth, which made me believe that whatever type of first birthday I'd had, it hadn't gone well.

What really freaked me out was the way my dad reacted. Usually when Mom was in the middle of one of her history revisions, he would meet my eyes and wink, letting me know he knew better. This time he went along with her without a look. I wasn't sure what he had to hide, but there was something.

chapter twenty-three

There is something very depressing about storage units. They're crammed full of stuff that people don't want to throw away but don't usually need. We're a nation of people who love our stuff, even stuff we no longer use.

We'd lost the key to the padlock on ours so many times that my mom finally hooked it to a giant troll doll key chain. Now we never lost it, even though it was ugly enough to want to. The lock clicked open, and I slid the corrugated metal door up. I sighed when I saw the stacks of dusty boxes. I had the feeling this idea was going to be a huge waste of time, but after my mom's latest lie, I had to at least try.

The storage facility boasted how everything was temperature controlled and well maintained, but I still wished I'd brought some rubber gloves. If I were a bug or mouse, this is where I would live. A giant mouse box high-rise. I kicked the bottom of the boxes to see if anything would scurry out.

"I come in peace," I called out to any hidden creatures. "If you leave now, we won't have any trouble. But if you wait and then run across my bare hands, I will kill you." I kicked the box again to show any possible rodents that I meant business. When nothing happened, I pulled the first box down and peered inside. It seemed to be full of kitchen gadgets, a blender that I was pretty sure didn't work, chipped measuring cups, cookie cutters, and a stack of recipes torn from the paper and, as far as I could remember, never made.

The next box down was full of books, including one on top on cultivating roses. There were two more boxes up front full of various car parts and tools. The entire storage locker was a fossilized version of our lives. If the box I was looking for was in here, then it was going to be buried at the very back on the bottom. I started stacking boxes in the hallway to clear some space. The dust from the boxes stuck to the sweat on my arms and face. I could taste the grit in my mouth. The last layers of boxes were taped shut.

I peeled the tape off the next-to-last box. Folded on top was the fuzzy bear costume I'd worn for Halloween when I was four or five. Underneath were more of my clothes. As I rustled through the items, I noticed that while my mom had saved a lot, there didn't seem to be any tiny baby clothing. Everything seemed to be toddler sized. I pushed that box to the side and peeled the tape off the last box. The first thing I saw was a giant box of Legos. I couldn't help smiling. I'd been a complete Lego junkie as a kid. Apparently my architect dreams had started young. I pulled open the lid and let my fingers run through the plastic blocks. There was something very satisfying about Legos, the feeling when they locked together. Under the Lego box there were a couple worn picture books. And then I saw the blue fur.

I shoved the books to the side and stared down at Bun Bun. He looked the way I remembered. He was clearly a well-loved stuffed bunny. His white paws and belly were a bit grimy, the powder blue fur had held up a little better. His right eye was loose. I pulled him out of the box. His left ear was nearly smooth. The nap of the fake fur was worn down from the near constant habit I had of rubbing it against my mouth. Clearly I was a kid with anxiety issues. My parents probably should have given me some Xanax instead of a stuffed toy.

I sniffed him. There was a hint of a peanut butter smell, but that appeared to emanate from a crusty patch on his back that quite likely was an ancient smear of Jif. I sat down on the concrete floor of the storage locker. It had seemed important to find Bun Bun, but now that I had, I wasn't sure why. He had been a long-standing, faithful friend, but at the end of the day he was still a stuffed rabbit. It was unlikely he was going to spring to life and whisper the secrets of my childhood to me.

Everything Brendan had said made sense. Bowton Island wasn't that big. If my parents had been childless and suddenly showed up with a kid, I couldn't imagine that would go unnoticed. This was the kind of town where the grocery clerk made a mental note of how much beer your family bought on a weekly basis, and the pharmacist would raise an eyebrow if an interesting prescription for a rash crossed his desk. Privacy was more of a vague concept here. People would insist that it wasn't gossip, but rather neighborly concern. The truth was, people liked to be in other people's business. It gave them a measuring stick to chart how much better they were than someone else.

In fourth grade I'd had a bit of a crush on my teacher, Miss Bauer. She smelled like freshly sharpened pencils, and every day she wore a cardigan sweater and matching colored tights. As far as my ten-year-old self was concerned, this was the height of fashion. After Christmas break she had returned to school with a diamond ring on her hand. She'd gotten engaged over the holiday to our gym teacher, Mr. Lumbardia. This had struck all the girls in her class as unbelievably romantic. We'd begged her for the details over recess and sighed as she told how Mr. Lumbardia had gotten down on one knee right at midnight on New Year's Eve.

I used to volunteer to stay after school and help Miss Bauer tidy up the classroom. My favorite task was to organize the three shelves of books we had into alphabetical order. In my mind, the books practically belonged to me. I felt like the official librarian, organizer of knowledge, and guardian of books. If I caught any of my classmates touching pages with sticky fingers or (oh, the inhumanity) breaking the spine of a book to lay it open flat on their desk, I would shoot them a dirty look. If that didn't work, I would rat them out to Miss Bauer. Books were serious business.

One Friday afternoon, alphabetizing long after my classmates had left for gymnastics lessons or visits with their divorced dads, I was stuck. There was a new book and the author had a hyphenated name, Barber-Starkey. I wasn't sure if the book should go under *B* or under *S.* It seemed to me to be a very big deal. I didn't want people to have to search for a book. The whole point of my task was to create organization out of chaos. I had a responsibility. If I could go back in time, I would pick my ten-year-old self up and shake her by the lapels and tell her that it didn't matter. Just stuff the book in anywhere and go home. Instead I took the book and went in search of Miss Bauer, who had gone to get something from the teacher's lounge.

I suspect if I had heard her talking to anyone else, I would have knocked right away, but she was talking to Mr. Lumbardia. I wanted to hear what she would say. I harbored a secret desire that she would tell him how I was her best student and clearly, as demonstrated by my volunteer activity, committed to organization, and as a result she wanted to ask me to be one of her bridesmaids. I could already picture myself in a bright pink bridesmaid dress, standing next to her at the front of the church. When I heard Mr. Lumbardia's voice, my hand paused just an inch away from knocking on the teacher's lounge door.

"I'm just saying, watch your purse on parent-teacher night.

Her dad has been in and out of prison so much he's got his name engraved on his cell door."

My throat seized shut. There was no doubt in my mind who he was talking about.

Miss Bauer laughed. "Oh, you're terrible. I have to admit, I was sure she'd be one of those kids with grime on their neck and constantly stealing supplies out of the closet, but she's quite sweet, and one of the better readers."

"Well, she's not setting the class on fire in gym. That girl couldn't hit a ball if her life depended on it."

"If you want to increase her running time, maybe you should make a police siren noise behind her," Miss Bauer said, before they both exploded with laughter.

I couldn't believe she'd said that. Miss Bauer with her matching cardigans and smiley face stickers that she would stick on my papers. I felt like I'd been stabbed in the heart. It was like discovering that your favorite fairy-tale princess is actually an evil witch complete with a hooked nose and broomstick. I ran back to the classroom and stuffed the book on the shelf. I vowed I would never volunteer another minute. Miss Bauer could organize her own shelves from now on. I was just about to leave when I stopped. I snatched one of the Judy Blume books off the shelf. Since Miss Bauer thought so little of me anyway, I might as well steal it. She'd already listened to the gossip and decided exactly who I was before I'd opened my mouth for the first time. She wasn't interested in my family history because she wanted to help; she was interested because it made a good story. It gave her some material to joke about with her sweaty fiancé. I'd shoved the Judy Blume book in my bag and run for the door.

I realized I was squeezing Bun Bun, with his ear held up to my mouth. I guess old habits die hard. I turned him over in my hands and noticed the tag sewn into one of his seams. The green print was faded, but it could still be read:

A HARRODS ORIGINAL—LONDON, ENGLAND

I stared at the label. Harrods. One of the most exclusive, expensive department stores in the world.

The queen shopped at Harrods. My parents most definitely did not. So where had I gotten the bunny?

chapter twenty-four

I tore through the hotel hallways, stepping around the stacks of luggage and camera equipment waiting for bellhops to deliver them to the correct rooms. Mr. Stanbury saw me, but before he could yell at me for walking around without a uniform, I dodged down another hall.

I burst into the Arbutus Ballroom. They had already done most of the setup. The tables had cream tablecloths and deep blue runners. Every place setting seemed to have at least three glasses and four different types of forks. Being really wealthy means you never worry about how many dishes there will be to wash up later. One of the maids was washing the windowpanes, ensuring there wouldn't be a single smudge to mar the view. I finally spotted Chase, standing in the corner with a clipboard, ticking off items. I wove my way through the tables over to him.

I touched his elbow to get his attention. "Sorry to bother you, but can I talk to you for a minute?"

"Hey, I've been trying to reach you." Chase smiled, looking happy to see me.

I melted. It was nice to have someone pleased to be around me. Especially when that someone was as good-looking as Chase. "Sorry. Things have been busy; my dad just got home . . . from a long business trip, so my mom's been organizing lots of family things. I should have called you back."

"Don't worry. This worked out perfectly. Here, I wanted to introduce you to someone." He raised his arm to wave across the room.

"I needed to ask you something," I said. I wasn't interested in making this a social call. I was glad to see Chase, but I didn't have any interest in acting perky and nice to one of his friends.

"Sure." Chase was distracted, still trying to get the guy's attention from across the room. "But Mr. McKenna wants to meet you, too. I told him how your group volunteered to do all the brochures, and he wanted to thank you personally."

My mouth suddenly felt as if every bit of moisture had been sucked out. I looked across the room. It was Mr. McKenna. He was laughing at something someone said and had already motioned back to Chase. It was just a matter of time until he crossed the room. I searched his face. He looked a bit older than the newspaper photos. It seemed if there was even the slightest chance that he was my dad, that I should be able to tell, that there would be something like an electrical charge between us, a connection of sorts. But there was nothing. I tried to swallow, but my mouth was still too dry.

What would he say when he saw me? I was equally appalled by the idea that he might recognize me as that he might not. I spun away from him and grabbed Chase's arm. "I need to talk to you now." I dragged him out into the hallway.

"Wait a second, don't you want to meet Mr. McKenna?" Chase motioned over his shoulder back at the ballroom.

"Not right now. I'm a mess. I've got dust and dirt all over me."

"He isn't going to care about that—," Chase started to say before I cut him off.

"I care. I'll meet him later, okay? I want to make a good impression." I looked around the hall, making sure Mr. McKenna hadn't followed us. "Do you remember when you told me about Ava and her stuffed bunny? Do you know what it looked like, or where they might have gotten it?"

Chase looked confused at how quickly the conversation was changing. "Where they bought it? Are you looking for a stuffed bunny for some reason?"

I wanted to scream with frustration and pull my bunny out of my tote bag and shove it in his face asking if he could identify it once and for all. Maybe I could have a bunny lineup like on the police shows, each rabbit holding an identifying number.

"No. I don't want to buy a bunny; I just need to know about the one that used to belong to Ava."

"I have a picture of Ava holding it on my computer. I was going to use it in the slide show."

My heart picked up pace. "Can I see it?"

"Now?"

I nodded, trying to communicate it was important, but without looking too desperate.

"Okay, but my computer is up in my room," Chase said.

I flushed. It was stupid, the point of this was to see the picture of Ava's bunny, but I couldn't lie to myself. I liked the idea of being invited to his room. If things turned out the way I expected, it would change everything. I wouldn't have to lie about who I was, because I would be exactly the kind of person Chase went out with. I linked arms with him and led him toward the bank of elevators. "Great. Let's go."

When we got up to his room, Chase paused right after using his swipe card to unlock the door. He raised one eyebrow and looked at me. "Be honest. Is this a ploy to get me alone to have your way with me?"

I managed a sarcastic grin to hide how awkward I felt. "Drat, my plan foiled, and right at the cusp of reaching my goal. I should have known you weren't that kind of guy."

Chase flung the door wide open. "Why didn't you tell me that was the plan all along? I wouldn't have wasted time asking all those questions." He winked. "And for the record, I'm exactly that kind of guy."

I blushed again. It was annoying. I didn't see myself as the type to get all flustered, but Chase flirted in a way that I wasn't used to. It felt like being in one of my mom's romance novels.

Chase's room was pretty standard for the Keppler Hotel. A king-size bed, a desk by the window, a giant armoire where they hid the TV from view, and a wingback chair in the corner. It was nice, even if it was a bit heavy on the floral fabric for my taste. I stepped to the window and looked out. His room was on the end, so there was a partial view of the ocean, but I had to crane my head to the left to see it.

Chase stood in front of the desk and flipped his laptop open. "Let me guess, having to see this picture is part of your international woman of mystery thing."

"Woman of mystery?" I said, making my way behind him so I could peer over his shoulder. His computer screen saver was a shot of him standing with friends at the top of some mountain with their snowboards. An image of me standing next to him in a color-coordinated designer ski outfit flashed through my mind. Sure, I didn't know how to ski, but vacationing in Switzerland would be a great place to learn. I fought the urge to move him out of the way so I could scroll through his photos faster.

"Do you realize how little I know about you? It's like going out with someone who's in the witness protection program, or was just released from a lifelong career undercover with the CIA.

You never talk about your family. You've never told me where you live. When you didn't return my calls, I realized I had no other way to get ahold of you. You could have dropped off the face of the world and I wouldn't have even known where to start looking."

"I told you, I had a bunch of family stuff." I shrugged, noticing just how close we were standing to each other. The fact that he'd wanted to get in touch with me sent a shiver down my spine.

"If I didn't know better, I would say you were playing hard to get. I'd love to meet your parents, see your house. I bet your mom is the type to drag out all of those old naked-in-the-bathtub baby photos to humiliate you."

I tried to hide the horror I felt at the idea of him meeting my parents. I could almost picture his face as he looked around the trailer. My mom standing there with the gray straps of her bra sticking out from the collar of her shirt and my dad sitting in his La-Z-Boy, which had an armrest reupholstered with duct tape, with a can of cheap beer between his legs. "Trust me. My mom isn't the baby photo type. Besides, you've been busy with everything here. I know you don't have a bunch of time to hang out."

"I'd make time for you," Chase said. "I had a great time when we went to Seattle."

I flushed. "Me too."

"So you'll go out with me again?" Chase moved a step closer to me. I felt his thigh just barely touching mine. My breath started to come more quickly. He smelled like a mix of shampoo and some sort of cologne that smelled like warm tobacco and vanilla. I inhaled deeply, which made me feel dizzy. He ran his index finger down the side of my bare arm, and a wake of goose bumps rose up in response.

"Um, sure." I found myself leaning toward him. I felt my muscles loosen like I might become a molten puddle at his feet. Chase cupped his hand behind my head and pulled me the last few inches. His lips were soft, like warm velvet. My mouth melted under his, and his kiss became more insistent. I felt like I could take one step farther and meld completely with him, cease to exist.

Chase pulled away. "Now that I know you care, you can see the picture." He bent over and clicked the mouse a few times.

I wanted to shake my head to clear the cobwebs. Chase had a way of turning his charm off and on in a way that gave me emotional whiplash.

"So for our next date, I'm thinking we should do a nice dinner. We can celebrate me surviving this event and that we met. Should we stay here, or take the ferry over to Seattle?" Chase asked.

"Seattle, I think." I glanced down at the screen, and the oxygen in my lungs froze solid. The picture was of a giant Christmas tree decorated with white fairy lights and Tiffany blue and silver glass balls. Ava was sitting cross-legged, nearly buried under a pile of professionally wrapped presents. She was holding her stuffed bunny tight under one arm, with one of his ears draped across her mouth like a blue mustache.

It was exactly the same as my stuffed bunny. The same color. The same style. The same worn ear. I could even see a hint of the small green label sticking out from a seam.

The stuffed bunny I had was Ava McKenna's bunny.

My knees went out from under me.

chapter twenty-five

Chase's arm caught me around the waist as I started to sink toward the floor, pulling me up. He'd assumed my stumble was some sort of girlish swoon. He pressed his mouth down on me, and I felt myself respond, but when I closed my eyes, all I could see was the photo burned into my retinas. Chase took a step back and pressed me down on the bed.

"You're beautiful," he whispered in my ear.

I could hardly hear him. The blood was rushing around in my head and it sounded like a roar. Bun Bun belonged to Ava. I was Ava. It didn't make sense, but there was no other explanation. I was Ava. I didn't know how my parents had done it, how they had explained my sudden appearance, or why they had done it, but there wasn't another option. Everything in my life had been a lie.

I felt Chase's hand slip under my T-shirt and slide along my ribs. His hand cupped my breast and his thumb ran across the fabric of my bra.

Whoa.

"Mmmm, Chase?" I said in between kisses. I started to sit up but slid down on the slick bedspread. His knee was between my knees, his weight pressing me down into the mattress.

"You smell like the ocean," he said, his mouth moving down my neck. His breath was coming quickly.

"Wait a minute," I said, but Chase showed no signs of hearing me. One hand was on my breast and his other started to fumble with the top button of my shorts. I put my palms against his chest and pushed. It wasn't that I didn't want him, but I couldn't think straight.

Chase pulled back and looked at me. His hair was sticking up. "Is everything okay?"

It's hard to have a conversation when someone has you by the nipple. I pushed myself up onto my elbows. "Um. I think we should stop," I said. "I mean, you have to be downstairs, and I've got stuff I'm supposed to be doing." It was a lame excuse, but there was no way I could explain that I couldn't make out at the moment because I'd just discovered my real identity. Something about knowing the people I'd always thought of as my parents had abducted me was taking my libido down a notch.

Chase rolled over so that he was sitting next to me on the bed. "Are you sure?"

I shoved my T-shirt back down. "It's just not the right time."

Chase sighed. "No problem," he said. "I just thought since you wanted to come up to my room . . ." His voice trailed off.

"I wanted to see the picture," I reminded him, but I felt bad. I had wanted to come to his room for more than that.

"Right. You're in the market for a stuffed bunny."

I had the sense that Chase didn't get turned down very often. I could understand his frustration. I was sending all sorts of mixed signals, but it would make sense when I could finally explain everything. I imagined his face when I told him the truth. He'd be shocked, but maybe excited, too. It was going to be a big deal, and it was clear he was close to the McKennas. Maybe our families would vacation together someplace like the South of France. Or he could be the one to teach me to ski. Chase and I could take long walks on the beach in Italy, or he probably knew how to sail, so we could go out on a boat. He'd always lived in that world. He'd be able to show me around, introduce me to people, and make sure I used the right fork. We would have plenty of time for kissing, and much more, once everything was out in the open.

"So, dinner day after tomorrow?" Chase asked.

"I'm not sure I can go out. There's some stuff I have to do." I needed some time to figure out what to do next. Should I confront my parents? Go to the police? Send a message to the McKennas?

"You know, playing hard to get sort of relies on the other person chasing you." Chase pulled himself up so that his back was against the plush headboard. "But if the other person gets tired of running, the game is over."

"I'm not playing hard to get or asking you to chase me." I felt the bite in my words. I could understand Chase being annoyed, but he was acting like I owed him something. Like he couldn't even imagine me not being crazy for him.

Chase raised both eyebrows in disbelief.

"I'm not. There's a lot going on in my life at the moment. Everything I'm doing doesn't revolve around you, or an attempt to play you in some way." I noticed that he still had his shoes on and they'd left a muddy smear on the duvet cover. "You should take your shoes off." I gestured to his feet so he could see what he was doing.

"Why?" Chase looked down at the duvet. "The maid will take care of it."

I felt my lip twitch. "Did it ever occur to you that the maid has plenty to do without you smearing mud all over everything?"

"No, it did not occur to me. The maid should thank me. If I wasn't a slob, then she wouldn't have a job."

I wanted to rip the laptop off the desk and hurl it at his head. I grabbed my bag off the floor. "I need to go."

"Come on, don't be pissed." Chase patted the mattress next to him. "We can rent a movie or something. Order room service."

"I told you, I have stuff I need to do." I stood next to the door.

Chase kicked off his shoes. "Look, does that make it better?

Or are you ticked because I implied you were being a tease? I didn't mean anything by it. I was joking." He noticed my expression. "I'm not saying it was a good joke; it was lame. Worse than that, it was rude. Give me another chance. I'll make it up to you."

"This may shock you, but this actually has nothing to do with you. I really do have to go."

Chase picked up the remote off the nightstand and clicked on the TV. "All right. See you around." He didn't look at me.

"I'll call you," I said, my hand on the doorknob.

"Sure."

I waited to see if he would look at me, but he stared straight ahead as if he were fascinated by the episode of *People's Court.* I stepped out into the hallway and leaned against the wall, hearing the door click softly shut behind me. I'd figured out who I was but still couldn't figure out other people. Some things never change.

chapter twenty-six

I spent the night sitting on the rocks at Keeper's Cove. I'd hoped the rhythm of the waves would be a Zen-like meditation that would help me sort out what to do. I said the name Ava McKenna out loud dozens of times, waiting to see if it would feel natural at any point, if it would eventually feel like it was my name, versus the name of a stranger. Would I be expected to go by Ava, or would I still call myself Sadie?

Growing up, I'd hated my name. I'd wished my parents had named me something more normal, like Jessica, Amanda, or Emily. I was the only Sadie in our entire school. Apparently my dad's favorite band of all time was the Beatles, so he'd wanted to name me after one of their songs, and my mom thought it was a neat name. I supposed I was lucky he didn't want to call me Eleanor Rigby.

My dad. My mom. I kept thinking of them as my parents,

but they weren't. It explained a lot of things. There had been plenty of times when I was certain I didn't fit into our family. But while it explained some things, others made no sense at all. I could almost understand the kidnapping if they had done it for the money, but according to everything I'd read, there'd never been a ransom demand. I didn't always get along with them, but I had never really doubted that they loved me.

I tried to picture my parents standing over a three-year-old version of myself, deciding what to do. Maybe the plan had been to ask for money, but the pressure from the police and media had been too great. They might have been afraid they would get caught. Or maybe they'd become attached to me once they took me and decided they might as well keep me. I'd never talked about that kind of stuff with my mom, but there was a chance that she couldn't have kids. You see daytime talk shows all the time with women driven mad by infertility. Weeping. Saying how they would do anything for a child. I vaguely remembered a few years ago a woman had taken a baby out of a grocery cart. The mom had turned her back for a minute to grab some cereal, or to fondle some melons, and when she'd turned around, her baby was gone. The woman had taken the kid, walked right out of the store, and driven home with the baby rolling around in the passenger seat. She might have even gotten away with it, except for the fact that someone in her family had turned her in. Apparently, she was so desperate for a kid, and when she saw that baby, she couldn't help herself.

I'd always assumed my parents hadn't had more kids because of my dad being in and out of jail. It was hard enough to afford even one kid, never mind a giant family, but maybe they couldn't have more. You would think, though, that if my parents were baby crazy, then I would have noticed by now. Neither of them ever seemed to coo and get all funny around small kids.

I'd thought of a few ways they could have explained my arrival. Maybe they kept me hidden at first so people didn't know right away. My mom's parents were still alive back then. Maybe they'd told my grandparents they'd adopted and kept me there for a while, waiting a few months for the fuss to die down before bringing me back to the island. I'll admit it was hard to believe, but stranger things have happened. People get away with stuff all the time.

I remembered one year when I was around six or seven, I'd started to doubt the reality of Santa. My mom woke me up late on Christmas Eve so I could hear the sound of Santa walking around on the roof of our trailer. I always got new pajamas on Christmas Eve. That year they were pale blue with penguins wearing brightly colored hats all over them. My mom smelled a bit like cloves and nutmeg from all the baking she'd done that day. She'd curled around me in the bed, tucking her feet under the blankets to keep them warm. The trailer shook with the heavy steps of the reindeer and Santa.

"And you weren't sure he was real," she'd said softly in my ear, her breath tickling me.

"HO! HO! HO!" Santa bellowed. I covered my mouth to keep from giggling too loudly and letting Santa know I was on to his location. I'd squeezed Mom's hand, nearly levitating out of bed with excitement. He was here! Santa!

Suddenly there'd been a loud BAM and the trailer had shuddered. Then came a scraping sound followed by a huge crash outside my window.

"Shit!"

"Santa just swore," I'd whispered to my mom.

Mom had leaped out of bed and rushed out of the room. I trailed after her. She flung open the door, and my dad was staggering around the corner, his arm hanging at a funny angle. There was a branch sticking out of his hair.

"Jesus, I nearly impaled myself on that damn bush. There's a bunch of ice up on the roof, and with this freezing rain it's as slick as snot up there. I took one step and my feet flew right out from under me."

"Dad, why were you on the roof with Santa?" I'd asked, appalled at the situation. I hoped if this was officially classified as naughty behavior, it wouldn't count against me.

"Uh, I was helping Santa unload his sleigh."

"Did you break anything?" Mom had asked.

"No, I don't think so. Just wrenched it good."

She'd looked over at me. "I think that's enough Santa excitement for tonight. Back to bed."

I'd turned to leave but paused at my bedroom doorway.

"Dad? Maybe you should leave that stuff to Santa. He's sort of a professional."

I didn't know why at the time, but my parents had cracked up. My dad must have been crazy to climb up on the roof in the middle of the winter. He'd done it so I would believe in Santa one more year. They did it because they loved me. No matter why they took me, what their plans might have been, they did love me. They both drove me nuts, and I never felt close to my dad, and while there were times when I was pretty sure they didn't like me very much, I never doubted they loved me.

They would go to prison for this. This wasn't the kind of thing that the legal system was likely to go light on. With my dad's record, he'd probably never get out; they would lock him up for good. The prosecutor might work some sort of deal for my mom, especially if she had been crazed with the need for a child. However, in terms of sympathy, the McKennas were going to play better on TV. They would stand in front of their house, Mr. McKenna's arm around his wife. She would cry, but not messy tears with red eyes. Instead they would be tasteful tears, slowly tracking down her face as they talked about how hard it had been not knowing what had happened to me for all those years. They would make sure the best lawyers in Washington were on the case. My mom had already used my college money to pay for a lawyer who was the cheapest guy in the yellow pages. They would have to rely on legal aid this time around.

The sun was coming up. I rubbed my temples. I had a massive

headache. I had only a few weeks before the money for school was due. I was so used to worrying about money, I couldn't imagine what it would be like if I never had to think about it again. With everything that was about to happen, I didn't know if I would even go to school in the fall. I couldn't imagine sitting in Psych 101 taking notes and staying up late nights with my roommate talking about who had a crush on who. I didn't need to make over my life anymore. It was already upside down. I had no idea what my life would look like. The future was a complete blank.

As impossible as it was to imagine what would happen if I went public, it was equally impossible to imagine not doing anything. I couldn't fathom not saying anything to the McKennas. Now that I knew I was Ava, I couldn't pretend that I didn't know. I wouldn't be able to look at my parents and have this huge lie between us.

I had to confront my parents.

chapter twenty-seven

My mom had the radio blasting classic rock when I got back to the trailer. She was dancing around with a dust rag, wiping things off and then giving a shimmy here or there. I stood in the doorway waiting for her to notice me. When she didn't, I snapped off the radio and she looked over, surprised.

She gave an awkward laugh. "I guess getting caught dancing is what I get for having the music on too loud."

"I need to talk to you," I said. "It's serious."

Mom stopped fussing with the dust rag and stared at me. The air between us felt thick with tension. "Okay. You want something cold to drink?"

"No."

"Well, I do." She poured a glass of iced tea from the fridge and sat down at our small table, pushing aside the stacks of catalogs that were always there. She would circle items she wanted, items she would never order. She took a sip of her tea and stared across the table at me.

Even though I'd been thinking about it for hours, I wasn't sure how to begin. I felt like I might start crying.

Mom reached over and touched the back of my hand lightly. "Sweetie, what is it? Are you pregnant?"

My mouth fell open.

She sighed. "If you are, we can figure something out. Your dad and I will support whatever decision you want to make."

"I'm not pregnant." My voice came out as shocked as I felt.

She leaned back in the rickety kitchen chair. "Well, thank god for that. I saw your face and assumed the worst."

"Look, I know everything," I said quickly, before I lost my nerve. Her eyebrows crinkled up in confusion. "I know what happened when I was a kid," I clarified.

Her breath hissed out like a balloon with a slow leak. "How did you find out?"

My stomach went into a free fall. I had been sure she would deny it. "Why does it matter how I found out? What matters is what happened."

"I hoped you'd never have to know." She reached for me, and I yanked my hands off the table. Her hands were shaking. "I knew there was a chance you would think less of us if it came out, that it would change our relationship."

"A chance?" Her understatement made me want to pull my

own hair out and run screaming around the trailer. "I think it's safe to say that this is pretty much guaranteed to change things."

"I know it must seem easy to judge now, but things aren't black and white. Hindsight is different. I know what I did was wrong, and I'd change it if I could, but I can't. Try to understand, I did the best I could."

I stared at my mom in shock. Did she actually expect what happened was somehow okay? "I can't believe you. I think I'm being very fair given what happened. I wanted to give you a chance to explain before I talked to anyone else, give you and Dad a chance to see a lawyer, or make any other plans." I didn't say what I thought was most likely. If she and my dad wanted to make a run for it, I wouldn't stop them. Maybe they could take new names and start over someplace else. My mom always loved to talk about going to Mexico.

Mom looked at me with disbelief. "A lawyer? Why in the world would we need a lawyer?"

I knew my mom could be a bit naive, but I would think having been around my dad practically her whole life, a few things about the law would have rubbed off. "Kidnapping is a felony."

Mom laughed, nearly choking on her iced tea. "What in the world are you talking about?"

"I'm talking about the fact that I'm Ava McKenna." I wanted to hurl a catalog at her face. It made me so angry that she thought this was even remotely funny.

"Ava McKenna?" She looked around the room like she expected someone to pop up and explain the situation.

"Are you going to try to pretend like you don't know what I'm talking about? What about the fact that you just admitted it?"

"You aren't Ava McKenna." She rubbed her eyes as if she felt a headache coming on. "I think we've crossed signals somewhere. We're talking about different things. Let me start over." She took a deep breath. "Right after you were born, your dad went to jail. I was on my own, trying to figure out how to deal with a baby and keep up with the bills. I was nineteen." She tapped the table with her glass. "Nineteen. I was so young I hardly knew how to take care of myself, let alone a tiny baby."

"What are you saying?"

"I'm not proud of any of this, you have to know that. I'm trying to help you understand. I wasn't sleeping much. I was so tired all the time. There were piles of laundry everywhere, and people calling about payments that were late for this and that. You were a fussy baby. There were times when you wouldn't stop crying until I felt like I was going to pull my hair out. Nowadays, they would probably figure out that you were lactose intolerant or had colic, but back then all you did was cry. You would lie there in your crib and scream."

I didn't say anything. I was still stuck at trying to understand what she meant when she said I wasn't Ava.

"I don't mean to make it sound like it was your fault. Babies cry, that's what they do. What happened was my fault."

"What exactly did happen?" I asked.

Her eyes slid away from mine and looked out the kitchen window. "I shook you. I wanted you to stop crying. I was so tired and you wouldn't stop. When I saw the bruises on your arms in the morning, it was the worst moment of my life."

"Someone else saw the bruises," I guessed.

"The doctor. He called Child Protective Services. They took you into foster care over on the mainland. I wasn't in a place where I could be a good mom, and your dad was in jail. They took you away when you were just a few weeks old. I felt like my entire world was crashing in."

"That's why there aren't any baby pictures of me." My voice sounded flat.

"You have to understand, I wanted you back, but social services made me jump through all these hoops. I mean, they were right to do that, but don't think for a minute I didn't want you back here. But it took a long time."

"I was three by the time you got me back, wasn't I?"

"Your dad brought you home. He'd gotten out of jail just a few days before. It felt like we were getting a fresh start at being a family. Maybe I should have told you as you grew older, but I was ashamed. You were so young, I figured you wouldn't remember any of it. Your dad brought you home the same day Ava McKenna went missing; that's the only connection between you two. I'm afraid you were born into this family."

My brain felt as if it had stalled. I wasn't Ava McKenna. "What about the bunny?"

"Bunny?"

"The stuffed rabbit I had as a kid. It belonged to Ava McKenna."

Mom pressed her lips together. "I was so excited you were finally coming home. I wanted everything to be perfect. I was working that morning. I was responsible for cleaning the McKennas' room that week. I was up in their room those days more often than I was home. They were always calling, wanting more towels or fresh pillows, more bubble bath. I must have run up to their suite a thousand times a day. Their daughter, Ava, had so many toys. Piles of them. The morning she went missing, they called up wanting more bath towels they could take out sailing with them. I saw the stuffed rabbit sitting there, and it seemed like the perfect thing. You could tell it was quality, not some cheap thing. She had so many toys. I couldn't see how it would matter. It seemed like you deserved something special."

"You stole the bunny." The last piece of the puzzle clicked into place. Brendan had been right: There was an explanation for everything.

"It sounds stupid now. It *was* stupid. If I'd been caught, I would have lost my job. Then when that girl went missing, the police were asking questions. They asked me about the stuffed bunny and I thought my heart would stop. I didn't tell them the truth. I was afraid I'd get in trouble. I hadn't even seen Ava that morning.

She was always off with her parents or that nanny. I didn't want to lose my job over something so stupid. God help me if that small detail would have helped them with their search in any way."

"But no one ever figured it out."

She looked at me. "No, they never did."

I felt hollowed out, as if my insides had been removed with an ice-cream scoop. I was an idiot. I had been distraught about having to send my parents off to prison. I'd prepared a speech for when I met the McKennas. It had been important for me to make a good first impression. I felt a hysterical laugh almost break free. What if I had gone to them first? Told them that they didn't need to be sad any longer, that I, their long-lost daughter, had returned. That would have gone over *so* well.

"I'm sorry," my mom said, breaking my train of thought. "I should have told you a long time ago about how you had been in foster care. I guess I didn't want to give you another reason to think I'm a bad mother."

"You're not a bad mother," I said, and I meant it. She'd only been nineteen, a year older than I was right now. I tried to imagine my life with a baby, bills, and no chance of escape. I wasn't even sure I could take care of myself, let alone anyone else. But at least she'd tried. She'd done the best she could, and then when she screwed up, she did everything she could to get me back. She'd done better than I could.

Mom stood and poured herself another iced tea and then filled an extra glass. She slid it across the table to me. "I am a bad mother, but not so bad that I don't at least know it and at least wish I had done better."

"It's okay."

"You know why I took your college money?"

"To pay for Dad's lawyer."

"No, that's the lie I told myself, and then you. Even as I did it, I knew that wasn't the real reason. I used the money for his lawyer, but that's not why I took it to start with. I said that because it felt better than the truth. I took it because I knew if you went away to college, I'd never see you again." She swallowed and her eyes filled with tears. "Moms are supposed to want what's best for their kids, but I didn't do that. I wanted you to be here. I took your money so you couldn't leave me." She looked around the trailer. "I wasn't going to keep you here by relying on the charm of this place."

"I would have come back to visit," I said. My throat felt tight, because I suspected she was right. I wouldn't have returned. My real life didn't go with the new life I'd been planning. I would have felt ashamed to invite any of my college friends here to meet my parents. I'd have been angling to get invitations from them for the holidays. Anything but home. She wasn't a bad mom. I was a bad daughter. Ungrateful. Ready to forget her and everything she'd ever done for me.

Mom patted my hand. "Nah. You would have kept running, and who would have blamed you? I didn't plan to get pregnant when I did. I guess that's no surprise; who feels ready at nineteen to be a mom?" She reached across the table and turned my head, holding my chin so I couldn't look away. "Even though I didn't plan it, I didn't regret it. I wanted to be the kind of mom you deserved, but I wasn't up to the task. It was so much harder than I imagined. I am sorry. I'm even more sorry that I stopped trying somewhere along the way. If I could tell you that you were Ava, and that you could have that kind of perfect life, I would, but I can't."

Tears started to roll down my face. "I'm sorry too. I didn't mean to make you feel bad."

My mom stood up. I flung myself into her arms and she squeezed me tight. "Look at us, a bunch of sad sacks."

I sobbed as I held on to her. It felt like a tight band that had been wrapped around me for years was suddenly gone. She rubbed my back and let me cry. She pulled away slightly so she could look at my face.

"I've screwed up a lot of things, but you know the best thing about messing up all the time?"

I sniffed. "No."

"If you're at rock bottom, the only way is up." She smiled. "You know what they say. Messing up just gives you a chance to learn something. Who wants to be a know-it-all? Much better to keep learning."

I rubbed my eyes. "I seem to be pretty good at giving myself lots of learning opportunities."

"That's how you know you must be my kid. We come from a long line of people who seem to need to learn the hard way." She rubbed a smear of mascara off my cheek.

chapter twenty-eight

I parked my scooter outside of Brendan's house. He was out front mowing his parents' yard. His shirt was off, and he was sweating in the heat. As he rounded the corner, he saw me and turned off the mower. He grabbed his T-shirt and wiped off his face. There was an awful moment when I thought he might turn the mower back on and ignore me, but instead he walked over.

"You know if you just mow over the dandelions, more will grow back," I said. "I'm sort of an expert in bad lawn care."

"Maybe I like dandelions. I think they give our lawn a bit of character. You came over to give me landscaping advice?"

"You told me when I figured out what I wanted I should come talk to you."

Brendan scratched his nose and avoided my gaze. "I was out of line. You should do whatever you need to do. It's your life."

"I just accused my mom of kidnapping me from the McKennas."

Brendan's mouth tightened. I could tell he was dying to hear how it went but was doing his best not to ask.

"Turns out, I didn't know nearly as much as I thought. I was wrong." I squeezed out a fake laugh. "Guess you saw *that* coming."

"Huh." Brendan's face was impassive.

"You'll never guess. I was in foster care as a kid." I didn't wait for him to react. "My mom lost it when I was a baby and they took me away. That's why there aren't any baby pictures. Far less glamorous than being a missing heiress."

Brendan didn't say anything but led me over to the corner of his yard. There were two old plastic deck chairs under a huge pine tree. He brushed the pine needles off the seat. I plopped down. It was cooler in the shade. Brendan sat next to me. He smelled like fresh-cut grass.

"I'm sorry," he said, looking down at his hands. His thumb rubbed a smear of dirt off his palm.

I sat up, surprised. "Why are you apologizing? I was a jerk. I'm the one who's been running around chasing after some kind of delusion. Look at me! I'm a princess!" I waved my hands above my head, making Brendan smile.

"I'm sorry that things didn't turn out the way you wanted. It was important to you to be Ava, and I made fun of that."

"Any rational person would have made fun of it. You were

right. I was all caught up in this fantasy where anything I wanted would come true." I rolled my eyes. "I'm an idiot."

"The thing is, I think you're awesome. Just the way you are. I like you." He looked over with a touch of a smirk. "Idiot bits and all."

I punched him in the arm lightly.

"I got mad because it seemed like you wanted to get rid of the real you, that you wanted to be someone else. And . . . I didn't want to lose you." Brendan shrugged. "I wasn't listening to what *you* wanted. I was thinking about what *I* wanted."

I felt my throat tighten. "It's okay."

"Not really. The thing is, if you love someone, you should make their happiness more important than your own."

My heart sped up. "You love me?"

Brendan laughed. "You're just figuring that out now? Maybe the idiot part of you is bigger than I thought."

My mouth opened and closed like a fish. I felt like there was something I should say, but the connection between my brain and my mouth wasn't working. "What about all those other girls?"

"That was me being an idiot." Brendan shrugged. "You're my best friend; you've always been my friend, as long as I can remember. But you always made it so clear that we're *just* friends. I've had a crush on you since seventh grade."

"Seventh grade?" I tried to think back that far.

"I remember my folks took us over to the fair in Puyallup.

You were wearing this pink sweater. I was too scared to go on the rickety roller coaster, so I was standing there waiting for you. I was eating this giant tub of caramel corn. The coaster went swooping by and I saw this girl on it and thought, *Wow.* Then an instant later I realized it was you. That's when I knew that what I felt for you wasn't just friendship anymore."

I tried to wrap my brain around that. "I had no idea."

"I'll admit I can be an idiot sometimes, but I wasn't stupid enough to go and tell you that I was crazy for you. You always planned to get far away from here, and me, as soon as graduation happened. You were making escape plans back in elementary school. I went out with all those girls because I thought maybe you would see me with them and wonder what you were missing." He shrugged. "Then we slept together, and I thought maybe something was different. It seemed like you felt something too. I know you want to leave, but I wanted you to want me to come too."

I rubbed my head. It felt like my life was a snow globe that someone had come along and shaken. Everything looked different and I couldn't find my bearings. "I was so sure I had everything all figured out."

Brendan waved his hand dismissively. "Having things figured out is overrated. You don't need to know everything, just what you want to do next. Don't let anyone rush you into doing anything."

"Were you always this wise?" I asked.

"Pretty much. There's a reason all those girls always wanted to go out with me."

"I thought it was because of your good looks and the cons you pulled on them."

"Well, there was that, too. You can't count on everyone appreciating you for your brains." Brendan's hand reached over and lightly touched my knee. "Are you willing to give us a chance?"

"What happened to not needing to figure everything out?" I asked.

"Totally different when we're talking about me. You should feel free to rush into something where I'm concerned."

I laughed. "You don't give up easy, do you?"

He turned so we were facing each other. "Nope. Not about things that matter. I wouldn't have given up, you know. I would have followed you to California, or halfway around the world." He paused, giving me a moment to change things, but when I didn't, he leaned over and kissed me. His mouth was warm and tasted like the cinnamon mints he was always chewing. It felt exciting and scary and good and . . . exactly like the right thing.

I pulled back and looked at him. "I've wasted so much time chasing after . . . I don't even know what. A dream? Some kind of fantasy of what I thought my life should be." I shook my head and looked around the yard. "I thought being Ava was so important, but it didn't matter."

"Don't be ticked at yourself. Think how many people don't get their act together until they're like forty, and their lives are half over. You're ahead of the game. You figured things out and you're only eighteen. At this rate, you could be president by twenty. If there was a role for world emperor, you'd have that in the bag by twenty-five."

"I'm pretty sure that it would be advised that someone finish college before taking on the job of president. Besides, don't you have to be at least thirty-five?"

Brendan blew off my answer. "Never mind the Constitution. You could fix that up next year, while you're nineteen."

"While your world domination plan has some appeal, I don't think I see myself as wanting to take on all that responsibility." I paused as if I was giving the situation a great deal of thought. "I might like to focus on having some fun for a bit."

"What luck! I think I can help you with that. I don't want to brag, but I've got the fun thing figured out."

"Why do you think I picked you?"

Brendan leaned in and kissed me. "I will do everything I can to make you as happy as you look right now." He kissed me again. We kissed until a loud boom of rolling thunder startled us. Brendan looked around. The sky had filled in with thick gray clouds. "Sounds like a big storm is blowing in."

My nose twitched. I could almost smell the rain and the electrical charge of lightning in the air. "Should we go inside?"

Brendan pulled back and put a hand to his chest. "Oh my, are you inviting yourself into my boudoir? Things are moving awfully fast." He fanned his face as if he were overcome.

"I meant to get out of the rain, not so I can put the moves on you."

"Well, that's disappointing." Brendan stood up. "I should try to finish the lawn before it starts coming down. If you want to hang out for a while, we can do something after, maybe catch a movie?"

"Do you mind if I crash for a few hours? I was up all night."

"Sure."

"Later we could do something. Tonight's the big McKenna family event at the hotel," I reminded him.

Brendan shoved his hands in his pockets. "Nancy Goodall checked in today, by herself. No TV crew with her." He glanced over at me. "I called to check. I didn't speak to her. I just wanted to know if she was here, in case you wanted to go forward with things."

"I wondered if she'd come."

"Do you want to go through with it? We still could. She'll pay to keep her lie from coming out."

I thought about it, taking in a deep breath and letting it out slowly. "No."

"It means you won't have the money for school."

"I know." I wondered what my future roommate, Cheryl, would think when she found out that neither me nor my matching bedspread would be there in the fall. A big part of why I'd wanted to go to Berkeley was to get far away, but I also really did want to go. "I'll see what I can arrange for this year with one of the community colleges. Then I'll apply someplace else. University of Washington is supposed to have a good architecture program. In-state tuition is a lot lower."

He smiled.

"What makes you so happy?" I poked him in the stomach.

"You design houses, you'll need someone to build them."

"I suppose you think you're the man for the job?"

Brendan flexed his arm. "Well, I am pretty handy."

"You're also pretty smart when you're not being a smart-ass. You should go to college too."

He smiled. "If you insist."

There was another crack of thunder. I bit my lip. "I don't need the money for school, but I still want to meet up with Nancy Goodall. Would you come with me?"

"Sure."

"Don't you want to know why I want to see her?"

"Nah." He grinned, gunning up his mower again. "It's enough that you want me there."

chapter twenty-nine

Tickets to the McKenna Family Missing Children Foundation event cost over five hundred bucks a pop. They weren't going to make it easy for the average person to slip in and join the party. Lucky for us, we weren't average. I practically grew up in the Keppler and knew the place inside and out. If there was a way to sneak up on Nanny Goodall at the party of the year, I could find it. I tapped my foot, waiting for Brendan to join me in the lobby. It was dumping rain, so he'd dropped me at the door while he parked his truck. I took a deep breath when I saw him dash in the front door holding the sports section of the newspaper over his head. He shook off and stuffed the now soaked paper into a trash can. I stood as he came closer. We'd dressed up in an effort to blend in with the crowd, but I was willing to bet we still would stick out. Both of us were lacking in the formal wear department. Brendan kept pulling on the sleeves of his suit jacket, and I was hoping my dress looked vintage and not just secondhand. I could tell Brendan wasn't completely comfortable in a suit, but he looked amazing.

"Take a seat," Brendan said, plopping himself down into one of the overstuffed chairs by the fire.

I shifted back and forth in front of him. "We should get going," I said. My goal was simple and impossible all at the same time. I didn't want to con Nancy Goodall out of her money; I simply wanted to convince her to do the right thing after all these years. She needed to come clean about what had really happened. It might not accomplish much, but it also might give the police a new clue that could lead them to Ava. I felt like I owed it to the McKenna family to at least try. I wasn't their long-lost daughter, but thinking I was had changed my life.

Brendan raised an eyebrow at my impatience. "Clearly you don't get to very many of these swank events. It's not even nine; this party will go on for hours. They didn't pay that much money to crawl into bed by ten and get a good night's sleep. We don't need to rush."

"Is there a reason we're waiting?"

"This is why you should stick to five-dollar cons," Brendan said, settling into his chair. "No patience."

"I keep telling you I'm giving up the con business." I continued before he could contradict me. "Yes, this technically counts as a con as I'm trying to con her out of information, but after this one I'm giving it up. If I need money for U of Wash, then I'll get it the old-fashioned way. I'll earn it."

"Old-fashioned, slow. Call it what you want. Either way, this is a con, and smart con artists make sure they know exactly what the situation is that they're dealing with before they go in." Brendan paused and pressed his hand to his chest. "I can't speak for you, but I'm smart."

"Fine." I dropped into the seat and looked around. "Are we casing the joint for anything in particular?"

"Watch and learn," Brendan said. He settled deeper into his chair, looking relaxed and comfortable.

I managed to dig up enough patience to last at least twenty minutes before asking him anything. Or maybe ten. Ten for sure. "So, have you gained any valuable knowledge?"

"As a matter of fact, I have." Brendan motioned to the front desk, where two of the maintenance workers were talking to the desk manager. "Given the storm, and the fact that there is such a high-profile event, I'm willing to bet the manager called them up to make sure the generator kicks on in case the power goes out."

"It would be a shame if the rich and powerful were in the dark."

"Indeed. It also means if we cut the power to the room for any reason, we shouldn't count on having a cover of darkness for very long."

I looked over at Brendan. "Cover of darkness? I wasn't aware we'd gone from talking to the nanny to engaging in a

Mission: Impossible type situation. Are you planning to lower me on wires above her?"

"I wasn't planning on it, but I like to know my options." Brendan motioned to the elevator bank, where I could see one of the room service staff waiting with a food cart. "Looks like they closed the main dining room. The café is open, but if somebody wants anything fancier than burgers and sandwiches, they're going to need either to be invited to tonight's event or to call room service."

I nodded. I couldn't see how this would be remotely helpful, but I hoped if I agreed, it would move things along so we could get started.

"The other thing I noticed is that there aren't any lights under Riker's door."

I glanced over. Next to the front desk was the office for Susan Riker, the night manager. Her door was shut and there wasn't any light sneaking out from under it. "That's weird," I commented. "Maybe she's sick."

"My guess is that Stanbury's working instead," Brendan said.

"He hates working nights," I pointed out.

"He also hates missing out on a chance to hobnob with the rich and famous. I'm guessing he didn't want to pay for a ticket to this thing so he made sure he was working so he could still go to the party. We're going to want to keep an eye out for him. He can't stand me, and you'll be on his hit list for being in the hotel when you're not working. Riker would give us a pass if she saw us, but he won't. The last thing you want is him busting in on you when you're trying to talk to Goodall."

"Is this where you want me to admit you were right about us taking the time to figure this part out?" I asked.

Brendan winked. "I knew it was right, but I like hearing you say it." He pulled out a pay-as-you-go phone. "Okay, I'm going to give her a call."

"Should we meet her in the ballroom?" I wiped my hands on the seat.

"Too many people and too loud. Plus, there's the chance someone would interrupt. I'm thinking we meet on the landing by the main staircase. They've got chairs up there, and it gives us the option that if we need to leave we can either use the main stairs, blend into the crowd of the ballroom, or take the back stairs. I don't think she'll do anything, but you never know how she'll react to being told we know she's a liar. My money is still on the fact that she lied to cover up meeting a boyfriend or just being stupid, but you never know how far she'll go to keep things under wraps."

I stared at Brendan. "You're really good at this."

"Nice that you finally noticed." He winked at me and then called Goodall and told her where to meet us. I forced myself to take a deep breath. All I could do was my best. Convince her to come clean by making her think I knew more than I did and hope that information helped the McKennas in some way.

I actually thought it was going to be that easy.

chapter thirty

Goodall was already waiting on the landing when we arrived. She was wearing a dark purple dress that was so tight it could have been painted on. She looked exactly as she appeared on TV, except up close you could see that she must apply her makeup with a trowel. It sat on her face like a thick mask.

"Ms. Goodall," I said as we walked up.

She sniffed in annoyance. She fished through her clutch purse and pulled out a Sharpie and quickly signed her name on a cocktail napkin. "There you go." She waved it in my face. "Thanks for watching. If you don't mind running along, I'm meeting someone."

I looked down at the napkin. She thought I was some kind of fan. "I wasn't looking for an autograph."

She touched her perfectly sprayed hair helmet. "I'm afraid I don't allow photos." She peered around me to look for someone else. I could tell she was fighting the urge to shoo me away like a pigeon.

Brendan stepped in between us. "We're the ones who called you."

Her face scrunched together. "You?" She looked at the two of us and then chuckled. "You're kids."

"Yep, you got us. A couple of annoying kids," Brendan said with a smile. "But we're annoying kids who happen to know you lied about what happened with Ava McKenna."

The smile fell off her face. "I don't know what you think you know, but I'm sure you're mistaken."

"There's no mistake," I said. She met my eyes. I felt a rush of victory when she looked away first.

"Now, I'm not admitting anything, but I'm also not interested in having my reputation smeared. Perhaps there's something I can do that would encourage you to focus your energy elsewhere." She brushed a nonexistent hair off her forehead.

"Why did you lie?"

"I didn't have anything to do with Ava going missing," she insisted.

"You didn't tell the truth about where you were when it happened, though. Don't you realize that any small detail might have made a difference to the investigation?"

She pinched the bridge of her nose as if to block out what was going on. "I didn't do anything to her. I was supposed to have the morning off; she wasn't even my responsibility."

"What happened?" I asked, my voice soft.

Goodall sank into one of the floral wingback chairs. "I was seeing someone; her name was Lisa. We were in that stage when you're obsessed with each other. With my busy schedule, we hadn't seen each other in weeks." She sighed. "Lisa called and said she was going to take the ferry over so we could meet for coffee. I was supposed to have the morning off, but then the McKennas were invited out sailing and changed the schedule."

"Couldn't you tell them you already had plans?" I asked.

Goodall laughed. "You've clearly never been a nanny. It's not that simple. They pay for live-in help because they want things in their life to be seamless. I was on call twenty-four seven." Her eyes went soft. "I wasn't planning to have some kind of wild reunion. I just wanted to see her. I got coffee and met her down at the beach behind the hotel back patio. Ava was running around picking up shells and sticks. She was going to build a house for her bunny. She'd had a meltdown that morning because I couldn't find that darn thing, so she had the idea that if she built a house, maybe the bunny would come back. I think either she wandered off looking for the bunny or someone lured her away with it."

"Did you see anything or anyone?" Brendan asked.

"No. I've played that moment over in my mind a million times. I swear she wasn't gone more than a minute before I noticed. She was playing on the beach, and then when I looked back around, she was gone. When I asked the hotel manager to help me, I fibbed a little about the details because I didn't want to explain Lisa. You can say people should be more open minded, but there are those who still don't think anyone who's gay should be around kids. At the time I didn't think it was going to be a big deal. I was so sure that we'd find Ava at any moment. When it became clear she was really gone and the police got involved, I couldn't suddenly admit I'd been lying." Goodall's lower lip began to quiver. I could see her fighting the urge to cry.

I felt my excitement deflate. I hadn't expected to feel sorry for her. No matter which way I turned in this situation, every time I thought I knew what to expect from people, every time I was sure I had it all figured out, I was wrong.

Brendan was looking at me, waiting to see what I wanted to do next. Before I could decide, I heard someone yell out my name.

I turned around and saw Chase bearing down on me. In his black suit, black shirt, and black tie, he looked like a vengeful crow. He grabbed my elbow and yanked me closer to him.

"You have some real nerve showing up here," he said.

"Let go of her," Brendan said, taking a step closer, his hands already fists. Chase dropped my arm but not his attitude.

"I did some checking, and there's no volunteer service club on this island. Imagine how confused that made me, so I talked to Mr. Stanbury, and he had quite a bit to say about your family and background. I guess you forgot to mention a few of those details to me. I trusted you, and everything you told me was a lie." His voice cracked and I realized he was hurt.

"Things were complicated," I tried to explain.

He looked over at Goodall, his lip curled up in annoyance.

"Let me guess, you've been looking for the highest bidder for the inside view of what's happened with the McKennas and you used me to get it."

"I'm not doing any TV deal. That isn't what this is about," I said.

"And I should believe you?"

"You need to back off," Brendan said. Goodall looked back and forth between us as if she were stuck at some sort of tennis match where one of the players might start whacking the others in the face with a racket.

"Chase, I'm not sure this is the time or place—," I started to say.

"If you've told Goodall anything, you should be prepared to get yourself a lawyer, because I can make sure you get your ass sued off."

I shook my head in disbelief. "You're not pissed, you're hurt. I don't blame you. I never should have lied to you."

Brendan stepped close to me. "Maybe we should go."

"Let me guess, you're not really cousins," Chase said, crossing his arms.

"Let me guess, you were always this much of a pompous asshole, weren't you?" Brendan asked.

Chase sneered, but he didn't say anything. He was right to be ticked. I'd used him to get the information I'd needed, but in some ways he'd used me, too. He'd only been nice because he wanted something. He didn't really have any interest in me.

Suddenly I felt exhausted. If I sat down, I wouldn't be able to get back up again; I would just curl up like Sleeping Beauty and not wake up for years.

"Let's go," I said, taking Brendan's hand. "We're done here."

"So you're leaving? You don't think you owe me an explanation?" Chase demanded.

I paused to see if there were any feelings of guilt or obligation left, but everything felt stripped clean inside. "I'm sorry about lying to you, but I don't need to justify who I am. I never did, not to you and not to anyone else."

There was a commotion by the entrance to the ballroom. Mr. McKenna walked out with his arm around his wife. Mr. Stanbury trailed just a few steps behind. Chase stood up straight and grabbed me by the elbow again as if he thought I might run away. Mr. McKenna stopped short when he saw Nancy Goodall in front of him.

"Jesus, just when I thought this night couldn't get any worse," he said.

He was wrong, of course. The night was capable of getting much, much worse.

chapter thirty-one

"I didn't come here to cause trouble," Goodall said. Mr. McKenna was glaring at her.

"Yes, you did!" Chase said, interrupting her. "Mr. McKenna, I'm afraid this girl used me to get information about your family so she could get on TV." I could see his hands shaking. "I thought she was someone else or I never would have talked to her."

"I keep telling you, I didn't sell any information. For someone who wants to go into communications, you should really learn to listen. Communications sort of implies a two-way street. I only came tonight because I wanted to help."

Goodall looked at me, her mouth in a thin line. She wasn't going to admit anything.

"If she's caused any difficulties, I can assure you that the hotel will take it extremely seriously," Mr. Stanbury said. He glared at me as if I had dragged dog shit into the lobby. It was looking like I was going to need to find another job to pay for my tuition. I had a feeling my employment at the Keppler was coming to an abrupt end.

Mrs. McKenna was staring at me, her face intense. She reached toward me. Her hand was shaking, just inches from my cheek. "Ava?"

I froze in place. She lightly touched my hair.

"You look just as I imagined you would," she said. I could feel everyone else focusing on the two of us.

"You're mistaken. My name's Sadie." I took a step back.

"I can vouch for her identity," Mr. Stanbury said. He didn't sound happy about the fact he knew me. "She grew up here on the island."

Goodall tipped her head to the side and reevaluated my face. "She does look like the age-enhanced photo, now that you mention it. Especially around the eyes. They say everyone out there has a double somewhere."

My heart was beating funny, as if it had lost its rhythm.

Mrs. McKenna reached for my hand. "Do you have the scar on your pinkie finger? When you were only a few weeks old, I pinched your hand in the car seat. It scared me so badly at the time. I couldn't believe I'd been lucky enough to have this perfect baby and I'd already managed to scar her. The doctor said by the time you grew up you would hardly be able to see it."

I pulled my hands back out of her reach. "I'm sorry. I'm not your daughter."

"We should go," Mr. McKenna said. "It was a mistake to come back here." He tried to guide her away.

"I always knew I would know you if I saw you again. The instant you were born you looked at me and we knew each other. It was like recognizing someone you've always known. You're a part of me." Mrs. McKenna's eyes burrowed into mine.

"I think she was trying to scam the family," Chase said. "Maybe she realized she looked like the photos. She told me a bunch of lies."

"She's the one who asked me to be here. The two of them practically threatened me." Goodall's nose lifted in the air. She could sniff a scandal in the making.

"Sadie hasn't done anything," Brendan said. I could hear the tension in his voice.

"I need to go," I said. It felt like the room was slowly being sucked free of any air. I couldn't catch my breath. It seemed I could take a step away and would find myself floating free in space, no floor beneath me.

"You have some explaining to do," Mr. Stanbury said, crossing his arms over his chest.

"You don't have to explain anything," Mrs. McKenna said. "Just come home."

I turned and ran. I bolted down the stairs, pushed past the crowd of people in the lobby, and burst through the front doors of the hotel. The rain seemed to sizzle off my hot skin. I didn't know where Brendan had parked the truck, but it didn't matter. I needed to run.

chapter thirty-two

We sat parked in Brendan's truck at Beeker's Point. Beeker's is a treed bluff overlooking the ocean and is the local make-out spot. Most nights a line of cars can be found parked along the dirt road like a drive-in restaurant where the only thing on the menu is nooky. Tonight the storm seemed to have scared everyone else off or they were afraid a tree would fall on their car, which could bring the mood down. You couldn't bring the mood in Brendan's truck any lower, so we seemed to be safe.

I stared out the front windshield. I'd been picking at my fingernails. The flesh down the side of my thumb was bleeding. My stomach felt twisted, as if I'd swallowed a ball of barbed wire.

"It doesn't necessarily mean anything," Brendan said. It was at least the tenth time he'd said this since he'd picked me up in his truck as I ran down the road away from the hotel.

"What do I do?" I whispered.

Brendan shrugged. "She's confused. She's been looking for her kid a long time and you do look like the photo. It doesn't mean anything."

"I have a scar on my pinkie finger." I said each word slowly, as if it were the first time my mouth had ever formed those words. "A small one."

"Lots of people have scars," Brendan said. I looked over. He was sweating.

"She *knew* me." I'd seen it in her eyes. She had no doubts at all.

Brendan sighed. His hands clenched the steering wheel, but he didn't say anything.

I lightly touched his leg. "It's more than that. I knew her."

The two of us sat in the dark truck listening to the rain bounce off the roof. "What do you want to do?" Brendan asked.

I leaned my head back against the leather seat. "My mom wasn't lying. I know she sometimes makes things up, but when she told me this, she was telling me the truth. Or at least what she believes is the truth."

"What did she tell you?"

"She told me that my dad brought me home from foster care that day."

Brendan sat up. "So we talk to your dad. I'll go with you."

"You don't have to do that."

Brendan turned over the engine of the truck. "I know."

We drove back to the trailer park in silence. The rain was

finally letting up. Brendan reached over and rested his hand on my knee. It felt like it was the only thing keeping me from flying apart. Part of me wanted him to drive faster so that we could be there and the whole situation could be over, and the other half of me wished we could drive for hours.

Brendan parked in front of the trailer, and I noticed my mom's car wasn't there. There were lights on inside.

"Do you need a minute?" Brendan asked.

I swallowed. "Nope. Let's do this."

My dad was pacing in the living room when we opened the door. He was shuffling a deck of cards in his hands. He turned around when he heard the door, but his face fell when he saw us.

"I thought you might be your mom. I hate the idea of her driving around when the weather's like this. She had a bridal shower for one of the girls she works with. I guess I'm not used to being the one waiting at home." He smiled at Brendan in the door. "You look like you've been walking around in the rain. You want a towel?"

"I need to talk to you," I said.

My dad looked back and forth between Brendan and me. "Is everything okay?"

"I met the McKennas."

The blood drained from his face.

chapter thirty-three

My dad rubbed his hands over his face. He sank into his chair. Brendan and I sat across from him.

"Your mom told you about the foster care, right?" he asked.

I nodded.

Dad sighed. "What she didn't tell you is that she was just sick about the whole thing. Losing you gutted her. It sucked all the joy and happiness out of her life. Whenever I called from jail, she was crying and I could hear in her voice that she was frantic to get our child back. She blamed herself, and if she didn't get that little girl back, then I thought there was the very real chance she would hurt herself."

I sat perfectly still, afraid that the slightest reaction might stop him from talking.

"There was nothing that woman didn't do to try to make

things right. She started taking double shifts so she could get some extra money to hire a lawyer to help us through the foster appeals process. They sent people out to the prison to talk with me. She put up with tons of interviews and home visits. They had her assessed by all sorts of headshrinkers. To be honest, I didn't think things would work out. People like your mom and me don't tend to measure up to society standards."

"But you got me back. You brought me home the same day Ava went missing," I said. I kept trying to put my world back on its axis so that things would make sense again.

"Your mom couldn't get that day off from work, and she didn't want to wait a minute longer for us to be a family. So we decided I'd pick you up." My dad gave a laugh that didn't have a hint of humor in it. "I hadn't spent any time with kids. I didn't know what the heck I was doing. Maybe it's easier to start with a baby, but starting with a toddler was a nightmare. I just about had a stroke trying to buckle that kid booster seat with the social worker watching. Well, whoever said kids find being driven around calming never drove around my little girl. Fussy and wriggling all around, like Houdini trying to break free. I decided to stop at the beach so we both could have a break, run around a bit. Get rid of some of that energy. Your mom wasn't due to get out of work for another couple of hours, and it seemed easier to keep a toddler busy at the beach than in the trailer." He looked around. "Never was enough room in this place.

"It's funny, you know. You make a small decision that doesn't seem important at all at the time and then your whole world turns upside down." Dad shrugged.

"Tell me about it," I said. I still couldn't tell where this story was going, but I felt as if we were walking along a cliff edge and at any moment we were going to plummet off the side.

"We went out to Seal Cove. I figured it was close to the hotel in case your mom could get out early, but it was also private, so no one would see me trying to figure out the whole dad thing. We weren't down there very long. Then bold as brass, this other little girl comes wandering up wanting to play. She was acting like she was some kind of fancy social director."

"Ava," I guessed.

My dad looked me straight in the eyes. "You." I swallowed. "You took Sadie by the hand and got her to help build a castle down by the shore. You were directing what could go where and what kinds of things Sadie could use. I could tell you were close in age to Sadie; you were the same size. You even looked a bit alike, but you could see the differences, too. Sadie was wearing something the foster mom must have gotten her. It seemed nice enough. I don't want to make it sound like Sadie was some kind of sad Cinderella in stained rags or anything, but little Ava, you could tell she came from money. Your clothes were just so and your hair had this fancy clip."

Brendan reached over and took my hand. He squeezed it so I could feel him there, backing me up.

"Course, at the time I didn't know who you were. All I saw was this little girl who wasn't even old enough to be toilet trained, and still had more than my kid would likely ever have. Heck, she was already the boss of my little girl, telling her to do this and that."

"So you wanted to take her?" I asked, my mouth dry, picturing myself as a pushy, bold as brass toddler.

Dad met my eyes, his face shocked. "No. I didn't want to hurt her." He paused. "You. It made me mad, but not angry, if that makes sense. It was obvious you'd come from the hotel beach. You came right through that little trail they have there. I knew you must have wandered off from whoever was watching you. Here my wife and I had to prove six ways to Sunday that we were fit parents, and your parents had just let you stroll off. Anything could have happened to you. It wasn't like I had a plan or anything. You just showed up, but once you were there I could see it was an opportunity." He rubbed his hands on his pants.

"An opportunity?" I said.

"I wasn't kidnapping anyone. You came to me, practically shoved yourself right into my care."

"So you thought it was okay?" I asked.

"No. I thought . . ." He stopped talking, as if he was trying to remember what had been in his mind. "It was clear you came from money. I thought there wouldn't be any harm in letting you play with Sadie for a bit and then I could bring you back to the hotel in a couple hours."

Brendan scrunched up his face. "What would be the point?"

"The point was I thought they might be so glad to have their little girl back they'd offer me a reward." He shrugged, looking embarrassed. "Sounds stupid now, but I didn't have a job, I'd just gotten out of jail. Any money would be helpful. I thought I could use that money to buy something nice for my little girl. Sadie deserved that. It wasn't like they were going to give me anything they couldn't afford. It wasn't hurting anyone. It was just taking advantage of a situation that presented itself.

"So I led you two girls around the point. I knew we'd be out of sight, but we weren't so far away from the hotel that if someone came across us, I wouldn't have an excuse to be there."

"What happened to Sadie?" I asked.

"You have to understand, I wasn't used to kids. I didn't grow up with little brothers or sisters. Both you girls looked small, but you were fast. One of you would run one way and the other would run the other. You, Ava, climbed up on a rock and then jumped into the water, making a big splash. You weren't scared of anything. Scared the shit out of me, though. I was hauling you out of the water when Sadie called out. She'd somehow managed to climb up higher. She was yelling at us to watch. She was going to show you. She was going to make a bigger splash." His voice choked and he paused to collect himself. "She slipped." He snapped his fingers. "Just like that. I swear I hadn't had her out of my sight for more than thirty seconds. That's all it took for her to climb up there and fall. She hit her head." He stared out the window in the distance. "I can still hear the sound of her head hitting that rock."

"She was dead," Brendan said.

"Yep. You wouldn't think something like that would kill a child. You think maybe a car accident, or if they fell out a window or something, but she didn't fall more than three or four feet. Even when it happened, I didn't think she was dead. I figured she was knocked out, but she was gone. I tried mouth to mouth, but even then I knew it wasn't going to work. There wasn't anything that was going to work. I hadn't even had her back for a full day and I'd lost her forever." He took a deep breath, fighting to keep control.

I jumped up. "So you just thought you would keep Ava? Oh, well, you didn't have that much time to get attached to Sadie, might as well keep this other one?"

He stood up and faced me, looking angry. "No. It wasn't like that at all. I'll admit I was scared. You were screaming and crying by then. I didn't have the best relationship with the police, and I had a little hysterical girl who wasn't mine, and a dead child who was, but that wasn't the problem."

"You were worried about Sadie's mom," Brendan said, his voice soft.

My dad fell back into his seat. His eyes were full of tears. "It would have killed her. For years she'd been talking about getting Sadie back. Ever since we'd heard that we'd regained custody, she'd been busy decorating her room and buying little outfits. It was all she ever talked about. I know it wasn't right. I've known it ever since that day, but all I can tell you is in that moment I panicked. I just had to do something."

"So you exchanged the girls," Brendan said.

He shook his head as if he couldn't believe what he was saying either. "I swapped their clothes. They were close enough to the same size. Sadie was so small." He swallowed hard. "I wrapped her up in my shirt and put her in the trunk of my car. I had a pair of shears in my toolbox. I cut your hair so it was short like Sadie's and then I took you home to your mom. Late that night I snuck out and buried Sadie."

Things clicked into place for me. "She's buried under that rosebush, isn't she?"

Dad's Adam's apple bounced as he tried to keep from crying. He nodded.

"That's why we never moved away, isn't it? You should have. It would have kept you out of jail and it wasn't like Mom was married to this place. She always wanted to go someplace else."

"She always talked about living someplace warm. You know how she loves the sun."

"But you couldn't go. Sadie was here." I sighed. "And Mom never knew?"

"She hadn't seen Sadie in over two years. You were crying for your mom, but social services had warned us there might be issues with the transition, so your mom chalked it up to you missing your foster family. She was so busy trying to make up those missing years. She had toys and cupcakes and all sorts of things she wanted to do with you. Sometimes I think she wondered if something was off, but she never looked too close. She didn't want to know."

"What about the McKennas? Did you feel anything for them?"

"Of course I did, but what could I do about it then? I couldn't come forward the next day and explain the whole thing had been a horrible accident," Dad said, his voice rising. "I knew I screwed up. I should have confessed first thing, but I didn't. It was the worst thing I've ever done in my life, but there are some mistakes you can't fix. There wasn't any going back. The only choice I saw was to keep going."

"What about the police? Didn't they ever show up?"

"About a week or so later."

"And they didn't notice?" I asked.

Dad smiled. "Didn't I teach you anything about why cons work? People see what they expect to see. Diversion. Everyone on the island knew we were due to get our daughter back. Your mom had told everyone she knew; heck, she told people she didn't know. Social services had been out and given us a passing grade. The day the cops came out to talk to us you were running around the front chasing Ms. Flick's cat. You were covered in dirt and cat hair. You had summer allergies, so you had that constant smear of snot under your nose. The cops looked right at you and then right past. You didn't look like a fancy heiress, you looked exactly like the kid they expected would be here. That was the end of that investigation. The only thing I had to be careful about was keeping your mom from taking you to the hotel. She wanted to show you off to all her friends, but I couldn't be sure how many of them had seen Ava. With your haircut and without the fancy clothes, they might not have recognized you, but I didn't want to take the chance. I convinced her it would be wrong to parade you around when that kid had gone missing." Dad shrugged. "Kids grow fast at that age, so after a month or two I figured you'd changed enough, and that people wouldn't likely remember anyway. People don't pay nearly as much attention as you might think."

"I don't believe this is happening," I said. I felt like I could pass out.

"That first year I kept waiting for someone to discover what I did, for the cops to come pounding on the door, but they never did. At least not about that. You grew up, our lives went on. Eventually, after a while, it seemed like you really were our kid." Dad shrugged as if the past fifteen years just slipped away from him.

"You never felt that though, did you?" I clenched my hands into fists. I couldn't believe I'd said that. I felt like crying and hated myself for having this needy "tell me your feelings" moment. I shrugged like it didn't matter. "You don't have to say anything. It was obvious my whole life that you didn't like me that much. I guess at least now I have a reason. I wasn't your real daughter and you knew it."

Dad reached over and touched my arm. "That's not true." He sighed. "I'm terrible at this stuff. It wasn't that I didn't care for you; it was that I knew what I'd done. You could have grown up with anything you wanted, and instead you grew up here, and that was my fault. It was never you, it was always me."

I knew he was waiting for me to say something, but if I opened my mouth, I would start crying.

My dad stared into my eyes. "I know I messed up. There were a million things you should have had in your life, but the one thing you never were short on was love. We couldn't give you what the McKennas would have, but we loved you just as much. I used to tell myself that was enough. I'm sorry for what I did. I've been sorry every day, but I'm most sorry if I ever made you feel I didn't want you."

I threw myself into his arms and he held me close. My tears melted into his T-shirt. He patted my back, and I felt as if I'd flashed back to when I used to fall off my bike and the only one who could make me feel better was my dad. After a few moments my dad pulled back and kissed me on the tip of my nose.

"What do we do now?" I whispered.

"I guess I need to turn myself in," Dad said. "If the McKennas recognized, you it's just a matter of time till the police come around asking questions. They might not think there's anything to the story, but they'll check it out."

My mind was racing. "They'll send you back to prison. You won't get out."

"You need to be the one to turn me in," Dad said. He held up a hand to cut me off before I could argue the point with him.

"Now that it's out, I can't ask you to keep that quiet. I never should have let this happen, but I sure can't ask you to hide my secret. I don't want there to be any chance that people see you as messed up in this or that you knew anything. You've been poking around the McKennas. If you don't come forward now, the cops are going to wonder what you knew and when. It's not worth the risk; they're going to get me anyway, and I want to keep you out of it."

"He's right," Brendan said.

Dad clapped Brendan on the back. "He's looking out for you. I like that." He glanced down at his watch. "You'll have to do it soon. My reputation is going to draw their attention pretty quick, especially if the McKennas are raising a fuss. By noon tomorrow at the latest they'll be here knocking on the door."

"I can take her to the police department now," Brendan offered. "It's late, but they're still working."

"I'm sure of it, but I need some time." Dad looked around the trailer. "I need to talk to your mom. There's no excuse, but I owe her an explanation."

"I'll stay and be here too," I said.

"No. I need to do this myself. You stay with Brendan tonight and go to the police in the morning. Tell them you weren't sure and were up all night going over the options and that you felt you had to talk to them. You don't know for sure, but you suspect I might have done something. They'll run some tests on you if I'm right. DNA usually takes a while, but the McKennas have the cash and influence to fast-track all of that. They'll wait to question me until they're sure about you. That'll give me the time I need. I want to have a beer, take a walk. Maybe I'll get your mom to make me some of her peanut butter cookies before they show up. I can't get enough of those."

"Okay." I sniffed. There were so many things he'd be giving up.

"Go grab yourself something to wear. You don't want to meet the McKennas tomorrow looking all wrinkled and in yesterday's clothes. You gotta keep up appearances now." He shoved me toward my room.

I clicked on my light and looked around. It felt like it belonged to someone else. It seemed impossibly small. I didn't know how I had ever managed to fit my life inside the space. I grabbed up my backpack and shoved a few things in along with some makeup. I turned to leave and then remembered. I opened the closet and pulled the stuffed bunny out. It was time for Bun Bun to go home too. I placed him carefully on top of the pile and zipped it up. Brendan and Dad stepped apart when I came back into the room. I'd interrupted whatever they'd been saying.

"Come here and give me a big hug," my dad said.

I squeezed him tight. "I'll come visit, I promise." I'd always tried to get out of visitor days in the past, but suddenly I realized I wanted to know him. Now that I'd discovered that he wasn't my real dad, he felt more like my dad than any other time in my life. No matter who I'd been when I was born, this was a part of who I was now.

"Tomorrow morning you'll become Ava again, but you'll always be my girl." My dad held my chin in his hand so I couldn't break his gaze. "I love you. Your mom loves you. Don't forget us."

"I'm not going to forget you. You guys will still be in my life. No one can keep me from staying in touch with you."

There was the crunch of gravel outside, and the three of us all turned toward the window. My mom was home.

Dad swallowed. "All right. You get out of here and let me talk to your mom." He turned to Brendan. "I'm trusting you. You take care of her."

Brendan stood up straight, as if he were in the military. "Yes, sir. I will." He took my hand and led me toward the door.

Mom dashed in shaking the rain off her jacket. "Oh, it's nasty out there." She smiled at the three of us. "What are you all doing standing around?"

Brendan stepped forward. "Sadie and I are just headed out."

"You sure you don't want to stay for a bit?" She dropped her purse on the chair and started bustling about. "It's getting late."

"You think those kids want to hang out with us?" My dad squeezed my hand before letting go. "You guys have fun."

Brendan nudged me toward the screen door. I took a step and then stopped and hugged my mom. "I love you," I said.

My mom started, surprised at my declaration. "I love you too, pumpkin." My dad put his arm around her.

Brendan and I walked out. I turned around and looked back at the two of them framed in the door.

"What was that all about?" I heard my mom say to my dad.

I followed Brendan out to the truck before I could hear his answer.

chapter thirty-four

Brendan drove us back toward town.

"Are we going to your place?" I asked.

"Nope."

"You thinking we're going to sleep in your truck? I know you love it, but I have to tell you it's lacking in the comfort department." I chucked a take-out wrapper that was on the seat behind me. I looked out the window. As we drove past other houses, I peered into the lit windows. You never know what is going on in other people's lives, but it seemed to me that no one's could be quite as messed up as mine. "The rain's stopped, but it's still going to be too wet to camp."

Brendan pulled back into the Keppler's parking lot. "Wait here," he said.

I put my feet up on the dashboard. It seemed like I should

plan out what I would say in the morning, but no matter how many ways I tried to approach the situation, my brain came up blank. I rested my head on my knees and might have even fallen asleep for a second when the screech of the driver's side door startled me.

Brendan held out a room key. "You planning on sleeping here? I'm thinking a hot shower and food is a better plan."

I folded myself out of the truck. "You're a genius. How did you score a key? You distract the desk clerk or nab one off the maid's cart?"

"I paid for it," Brendan said. He laughed at my expression. "It's a strange day. If you can be an heiress, I can go straight for once."

The beep of the automatic lock clicked the room door open. Brendan flicked on the lights and then crossed to pull the curtains shut. He opened the closet and tossed me one of the complimentary terry cloth robes. "You can take a shower first and I'll order up some food."

I stood under the shower and used almost all of the rosemary mint body wash until I started to feel human again. When I came out, Brendan was sitting on the bed. He motioned to the tray that room service must have delivered.

"I ordered the turkey club you like," he said.

I didn't think I was hungry, but as soon as I smelled the bacon on the sandwich, my stomach roared to life. "You got cheesecake, too," I mumbled around my mouthful of food. I sat down cross-legged at the end of the bed and inhaled the sandwich.

"This is the kind of situation where it seemed I shouldn't hold back on the dessert."

"You want half?" I asked him, pointing to the dessert.

"Nope. It's all yours."

I waved a forkful of cheesecake in his direction. "It has strawberries. . . ." He shook his head no. His face was serious. "You okay?" I asked, putting the dish down and pulling myself up so I was sitting next to him.

"Me? I'm worried about you."

I paused to think about it. "I don't know what I feel. It seems like everything I knew is upside down and inside out. It feels like we're in this holding pattern, like we put life on pause. Everything will come down to what life was like before and what it will be like after tomorrow."

Brendan's hand picked at the duvet. "You think you'll move to Seattle with the McKennas?"

I leaned back against the headboard. "I don't know. I can't imagine it, but I guess I won't stay here, either."

"They'll have the money to send you to Berkeley; I guess that's the silver lining." Brendan laughed. "Heck, they could probably afford to send you to college in France if you wanted."

"I think the fact that I don't speak French might be a problem."

"Nah. They'll hire a translator, some guy named Pierre or

something, to follow you around." Brendan started talking in an over-the-top French accent. "Oooh, mademoiselle, allow *moi* to feed *vous* croissants while we cruise slowly down the Seine River."

I smacked him with a pillow. "You sound like Pepe Le Pew. I'm not going to France."

"Things will be different though. You're going to travel all those places you wanted to go. Start hanging out at polo matches and carrying a purse made out of rare yak hide."

I looked at him. "Do you really see me as the type to go to polo matches?"

"But you won't be Sadie; you'll be Ava."

"It'll be me." I took his hand. "I'm not changing."

"You might want to. Why would you want anything to do with this place when you could move on?"

"It's not about this place. It's about the people in it. It's about you. You can't get rid of me that easy." I sighed and let myself think about the possibilities. It felt like standing on the roof of a giant high-rise and leaning over the railing to look down. I tried to find something to hold on to. "I might go to school. Berkeley wasn't just about getting away. I really wanted to go. College is a good plan. . . ." My voice trailed off.

"Are you asking me what I think?"

I shrugged.

"You've talked about wanting to go to school forever, and Berkeley's rated pretty high."

"I didn't know you were checking out the college rankings," I said.

"I know all kinds of things. There are buildings waiting to be designed after all, and I'm pretty sure that isn't the kind of thing you should wing."

I looked over to see if he was joking, but he wasn't. "You were right. If I design them, someone will have to build them. You know, California isn't that far away."

"There is no place you could go that would be too far away. Heck, I'd follow you around France if I had to."

"Well, and with that great French accent you've got, you would fit right in. Near as I can tell, you've practically got the language mastered." I smiled. "You're stuck with me." I leaned over and kissed him. "That's an order."

"Wow, your dad said you were pushy as a toddler, and you're still pushy," Brendan joked.

I whacked him. "I'm not pushy. Besides, even if I am, you have to take the good with the bad. You have to take the whole package."

Brendan leaned over and kissed me deeply. "You've got a deal." His hand ran down my side, and I felt my skin shiver as if each inch of me wanted to reach up to be closer to his touch.

I pressed my hand against the muscles of his chest. I could feel the steady thump of his heart. Brendan wove his hands in my hair and kissed me softly down the arch of my neck. My pulse picked up speed to match his. I pulled him closer to me, liking the feeling of his weight on me. Our kisses picked up urgency, as if we were running out of time. Our bodies knew everything would be different in the morning and didn't want to waste a second.

Brendan pulled back, his face flushed. "I didn't mean to pressure you." He swallowed. "I got a room with two beds."

"Do you want me to get in the other bed?" I asked.

"That's not a fair question," he said. His eyes were locked on to mine. "I'm trying to be a gentleman."

I reached over and clicked off the lamp. There was still enough light to make out his face. "I fell in love with you, so there's no point in you changing to be a gentleman now." I stood up and slipped my robe off, letting it fall to the floor.

Brendan let out a soft moan and pulled me back down into bed.

chapter thirty-five

I flipped the visor down in Brendan's truck and stared at my expression in the tiny mirror. I'd spent more time on how I looked this morning than I had when it had been time to take my senior pictures. I tucked a piece of hair behind my ear. I hadn't been able to eat the breakfast Brendan had ordered. It felt like anything I put in my stomach would bounce right back out. I pressed my lips together. I couldn't decide if I was wearing too much makeup or too little. I'd washed my face and redone it four times this morning.

"You look great," Brendan said. He kissed me on the neck and leaned over to look into the reflection with me. "You ready?" His hand rested on the door handle, and my heart sped up.

"Wait!" I cried out, grabbing his arm. My heart was beating

fast enough it could fly right out of my chest. I didn't want to get out of the truck. I wanted to stay inside forever.

"It'll be okay. You just take this one step at a time."

"Everything changes from this point forward." My throat tightened. "I feel like I've never been so alone in my whole life."

Brendan took my hand. "Not everything is changing. I'm not changing."

We sat in the truck, not saying anything. I let myself breathe in his calm until I felt that I had myself under control.

"Let's do this," I said. I stared through the windshield at the police department. There were a few people bustling in and out of the building, but overall it seemed quiet. I wondered how long it would take for the news to spread. I wondered if they would drag my dad in handcuffs in front of a bank of TV cameras in time for the evening news.

"Hang on a minute," Brendan said. "I have to talk to you about something." He chewed on the corner of his lip, which made me want to do the same. "I've been thinking about your dad."

"What about him?"

"I think there's a reason he wanted us to wait until morning to come here."

"He needed to talk to my mom," I reminded him. "I also think he wanted a night with her, a bit more time where he was free. He isn't going to get out of jail this time."

"I don't think he's planning to go to jail."

I wondered if Brendan was so sleep deprived that he was delusional. "It's not really up to him."

"I think he wanted us to wait because I think he was going to take your mom and make a run for it." My heart paused in between beats. "He asked me last night when you were packing if my dad still kept his fishing boat down by the marina."

"It's been a good twelve hours since we left," I said, looking at the clock on the dash.

"They could get a long way in that time." Brendan rested his hand on my knee. "I don't know for sure. I just kept thinking about him asking about the boat out of nowhere, and then when I thought about what he said last night, I realized he never said he was going to jail. He sort of talked around it."

I mentally replayed our conversation. Brendan was right. He hadn't just said good night, he'd been telling me good-bye.

"Are you mad?" Brendan asked. "I don't think he said anything because he didn't want you to have to choose between him and your mom and the McKennas. I might be wrong; I could be making a mountain out of a molehill."

"I don't think you're wrong."

"Your mom might not have gone with him," Brendan said.

I had an image of my mom with a scarf tied around her hair to keep it from blowing around as my dad guided the fishing boat across the water. I pictured them holding hands and I smiled. My dad knew people, not always the best people, but people who would know how to get fake identification. If they played their cards right, they could be in Mexico by tomorrow. "I bet she went. I hope she did."

I opened the door to the truck and waited for Brendan to join me. He held my hand and we faced the station. "Okay. You ready?"

I nodded. We walked up the stairs. As we got closer I could make out the officers bustling around inside. I saw the McKennas sitting in the corner. I'd called ahead and told the police I had to talk to them about Ava McKenna, so someone at the department must have told them something was up. Mr. McKenna was drinking out of a Styrofoam cup. Mrs. McKenna was wearing his suit jacket over her dress. Her head rested on his shoulder. Mr. McKenna looked up as the bell rang when we opened the door. Mrs. McKenna stood up. She smiled and opened her arms.

I looked at Brendan. "I'm ready."

He squeezed my hand and we walked forward. No going back.

acknowledgments

The person who gets the first thanks is you. Feel free to write your name here ________________ and then show all your friends and family. Thanks for picking up this book. I know there are a zillion things you could (and maybe should) be doing, so I appreciate your spending the time reading this book. To all the readers who showed up at signing events, conferences, told your friends they had to read my books, or took the time to e-mail, you made my day.

I can't imagine a better team to work with, so I need to thank everyone at Simon Pulse. I adore my editor, Anica Rissi, more than cupcakes, and that's saying a lot. To Roogie, my editorial dog, extra liver treats. Also big thanks to Jennifer Klonsky, Angela Goddard, Michael Strother, Mara Anastas, Bethany Buck, Anna McKean, Amy Jacobson, Lauren Forte, Annette Pollert, and everyone else who works so hard to take my ramblings and form them into the book you're now holding. To my agent, Rachel Coyne, thanks for the million things you do, not the least being talking me off the ledge when I need it.

To all my friends and fellow writers—I couldn't do this without you. For every time you cheered me on, celebrated a success, or told me to pull up my big girl panties and stop whining—thanks. Appreciation also goes to my family. They continue to read my books and are proud of actually being related to me, in particular my dad and aunt Joanie, who flog my books when they are on vacation. If someone on a cruise or in a tourist trap tries to shove a book in your hands, then say hi to my family.

Lastly, thanks to Bob. I make stuff up for a living, and I couldn't imagine a better person to have in my life. To my dogs, stop digging holes in the yard. No use blaming it on the neighbor's cat; I can see you from my office window.